PLEBEIAN IN DANGER

BY

DEBBIE K. LUM

Library of Congress Control Number: 2016900390

DKLit, LLC, Tampa, Florida

ISBN: 978-1-944463-01-4

Cover design and interior formatting by Deborah Bradseth of Tugboat Design

www.debbielum.com

Acknowledgments

Writing a second book doesn't get easier. But it does give you another reason to pull more friends in for the ride!

Thank you to Carl, Alexander and Ashton and the following friends.

Karen Cowan for your sharp words and highly specialized expertise. Thanks for letting me keep the necklace.

Trent Downing and your rock-n-roll wisdom.

Keri Kiefer Riegler and Amber Marcellino for your eyes and opinions.

Mandy Schoen for not laughing at me when I said I had another book to edit.

And Jill Reagan Healey: Your encouragement made me dig deeper, think weirder, and go someplace I never imagined I'd go.

Enjoy your hunt for limes.

[ONE]

Under the bright lights of a stark hospital room, it's hard to look good. And right now Plebeian guitarist Max Burgess looks horrible.

"I can't believe this happened to him." Lauren Hayden, the lead singer, squeezes their injured member's hand.

Guitarist Johnny Fulton stands over Max's bruised, sleeping body. "He looks like crap."

"Why do you think this happened?" Lauren asks, looking for answers in Johnny's worried eyes. No matter how much time has passed, she still trusts what her ex-boyfriend thinks.

He tilts his head to get a better view of Max's face. "Random stage accident. It had to be."

She nods. *Had to be.*

Dinging tones from the hospital's paging system disturb Max's sleep and he begins to stir.

"He's waking up…should we go get the other guys?" Johnny asks.

"No, let's keep it quiet in here," Lauren says, stroking Max's hand. "You and I can break the news to him."

Johnny runs his hands through his thick, black hair. Normally, watching when he does that unleashes a few old butterflies in her stomach. But now, her stomach is too busy churning with nerves.

Max's eyes blink open.

"Hey…" Max says, eyelashes fluttering as he tries to focus. "You guys are here?" His unwieldy, curly blond hair moves with his awakening, looking as traumatized as his body.

"Of course! You knew we'd come right after the concert," Lauren says, squeezing his hand.

"Hey, you look great!" Johnny says, lying to give Max an emotional lift. Plebeian is about to leave him behind to continue their world tour.

"I'm so sorry, you guys. I can't believe I fell. I just got in the band! We just started the tour!"

"You didn't fall; the stair unit did," Johnny says. "Not your fault."

"They are trying to figure out what happened," Lauren says. "And at least it's just a broken leg…plus a couple bruises." She hopes her reassuring smile will distract Max from asking for a mirror.

"I'm gonna miss you, Chipper! You've been my best buddy on tour."

Lauren runs her fingers through Max's curls, using the same caring touches she'd use if one of her own sons were lying here. Max has been her best buddy too.

The door opens and Lauren snaps her glance to see who is coming in. A chubby doctor enters the room.

"Ah! The others from the American rock band Plebeian," he says, his words dripping with a thick German accent. "I need to take a look at your friend here."

Lauren stops organizing Max's curls. "Hang in there, okay? I'll call as soon as we get to the next gig."

His eyes look as hurt as his body must feel.

Johnny and Lauren step into the hallway where the others are waiting.

Band manager Davis Perkins looks up from his phone. "Max's sister is on the way. We'll have someone stay here in Berlin until she comes." Davis wears his standard blue boat shoes and plaid shirt and goes back to fiddling like he always does with his phone.

"Was Max okay?" asks keyboardist Michael Casper. Usually Michael wears a daring smile, his bright, white teeth offset by the dark skin of his African-American complexion. But lately, Michael hasn't been smiling much, at least since they've been on this tour.

Bassist Oliver Brinks leans in, two bony fingers scratching his sweaty, matted brown hair. "What kind of question is that? The kid's dreams have just been crushed."

Doug Maggio, their short, quiet drummer glances at Oliver and frowns.

"This isn't ideal but we went three years without a permanent third guitar player. We can finish the tour using backups," Johnny says.

"This voodoo world tour," Oliver says.

"No kidding," Michael says. "We've had our share of bad luck. It's a miracle this tour even happened since Robert died. Under sketchy circumstances."

"You've gotta stop, Michael," Lauren says, lowering her voice and looking over her shoulder. "Mischief has never been proven."

"Right. A rich, healthy record producer drives his car over a cliff; it happens every day."

"You better not let Max hear you talk about his dad's death like that. What has gotten into you?"

"I've got a case of common sense," Michael says. "We announced a world tour and then you got shot. Next, our producer and record company president's dead body was found at the bottom of a canyon. Now, our new guitarist falls six feet, along with the staircase he was climbing."

"Not related," she says. "Crazy fan. Bad car brakes. Freak stage accident."

Oliver's mouth widens in a sarcastic smile. "I'm surprised with all this bad luck you haven't run."

"Look, I'd rather be home with Andy than be on stage," Lauren says. "But we all signed with Platinum Plate to do this tour. Even two bullets in my chest weren't enough to cancel."

Johnny nods towards a man walking their way. He huddles the five closer. "Here comes Shane. Maybe he'll know what the hell happened."

Shane Mitchell is a welcome sight to Lauren. He has been involved with Platinum Plate since Plebeian laid their movie soundtrack, one of the trusted few who knew the band before they were revealed.

"Oh goodie," Michael snarls. "We need our new record company president to tell us about us."

Lauren glares at Michael again. Why is he so snarky lately? "Gee, Michael. Shane may be new to his position but he's been around us since the beginning. He *is* one of us!"

Michael shakes his head.

"How's Max?" Shane asks, his sandy brown hair fashionably spiked and a swoon-worthy smile spread across his tanned face. He holds a coffee cup in each hand.

"Broken leg," Davis answers. "We'll have to move on without him."

"That's not good. Is Frank back with any news?"

"Not yet and I wish he'd hurry," Lauren says, scanning the empty hall.

"You okay?" Shane leans towards her.

"Not really. I'm gonna miss Max."

"Here. For you." Shane offers her one of the cups. "It's hot tea, one cream, no sugar—just like you and Max would share."

"Awww…thanks." She takes the tea and a drawn-out sip. Max always insisted she drink something warm to soothe her throat as soon as she got off stage. As her vocal coach, Max spent months after the shooting working with her on breathing and vocals. "How'd you know how I take my tea?"

Shane smiles. "I've been around you long enough to know these things. I can't take Max's place on stage but at least I can get you tea. The only thing I won't do is call you Chipper."

"Thank God," Oliver says, turning to Lauren. "Why in the hell did Max keep calling you Chipper?"

She rolls her eyes in Oliver's direction. "Somewhere in this hospital there must be a vial of poison for you to swallow." If she had a few spare minutes, she'd lead the search to find it.

Another approaching man draws their attention. *Finally!* "Frank!" she calls to her head of security. "Thank goodness you're here."

"Find out anything?" Shane asks as Frank reaches their group.

Frank Allen stops and brings his hands to his hips, his blazer parting slightly to show his new 24/7 accessory: a holster with a gun. Since Lauren was shot, Frank rarely leaves her side and is never without his weapon.

"The crew insists the stair unit was clamped to the platform properly," Frank says. "They went up and down that back staircase a hundred times setting up. They were searching the broken pieces for a clue but had to get out of the arena and get the trucks moving."

"Speaking of moving, we've got to go," Davis says. "Charter flight is waiting."

"Now? I'm not wearing these sweaty clothes all the way to Paris," Oliver says, tugging his wet, white t-shirt.

"Tough it out," Michael says, drawing another skeptical look from Lauren.

The group begins a slow, rambling walk down the long hospital hall, leaving their youngest member behind. Just the smell of this hospital makes Lauren's chest hurt. With every step she cautiously surveys everything she passes. Open doors to patient rooms, abandoned equipment in the hall, paperwork piled on the nurse's desk. Her sweeping glances expose the fear in her eyes while her straight brown hair pulled back in a sweaty ponytail gives her nothing to hide behind. Even though she's not a patient lying in a hospital bed anymore, she still feels like she's recovering. The shooting she suffered from a stalker has made it harder for her to do most things. She needs deeper breaths to fill her scarred lungs to sing. She tires easily. Simple things frighten her now. But she's here, on tour. She lived to make it.

Their wait by the elevators gives Lauren something new to notice: a wall plaque dedicating this hospital wing. She can't translate the German words but can read the letters of this city: Berlin.

"How ironic is this," she whispers to Johnny, who is never far from her side. "Last time the city of Berlin was involved in my life it started a series of upheavals that ended with me in the hospital. Now here I am, standing in a Berlin hospital."

Johnny smiles and nods. "Your ex-husband's wild evening in Berlin led you to Andy, and then you were hit by a drunk driver, which led Andy to party like a madman and ultimately led a madman to shoot you because he thought he was Andy."

She grimaces. "I hope this isn't the beginning of more upheaval."

[TWO]

"Lauren, please," Frank asks again. He fidgets in the front passenger seat of the SUV. Their French driver taps the steering wheel, his foot hovering over the gas pedal.

They are the lead vehicle in this caravan and if they don't get moving in a few seconds they'll get stuck in departing concert traffic.

"We've got to go. Now…" Frank says again.

A car horn beeps behind them.

Frank is out of time and patience.

"*Lauren*, please dismount your husband *now*," he says. "*Andy*, remove your wife from your lap and *both of you* buckle your seatbelts!"

Lauren's giggles mean her mouth is off Andy.

"Gotcha, Frank," Andy says. Two clicks.

Frank turns to see Lauren in the middle, buckled, and Andy beside her, buckled, both wearing shit-faced happy grins.

"I know you haven't seen each other in a while but you know we never roll without seatbelts. Not since Dallas," Frank says.

"Thanks, Daddy," Lauren says.

Their SUV accelerates quickly, the speed of their departing turn pushing Andy's face into Lauren's sweaty hair.

"Mmmm…look what I found," he says and kisses her.

The driver glances at Frank, who shrugs. "See why no one wanted to ride with us?"

* * *

"Get your body in my bed," Lauren says, peeling back the sheet.

Andy steps from the steamy bathroom, his hair gloriously wet and messy, a towel draped around his neck. Water droplets bead on his tight abs after their shower together. "Oh, look who's all bossy now," he says with an edgy grin, throwing his towel to the floor and sliding in.

She rests her head of wet hair on his bare chest and rubs his stomach dry. "You had your way with me, twice. Now it's my turn."

He wraps his arms around her. "And what did you have in mind?"

"This." She squeezes him. "Snuggle me."

"Anytime; anywhere," he whispers. His warm hold melts away her stress, her fear, her sadness. Oh, how she has missed Andy Hayden.

Their bare bodies are lost under the white down softness; the oversized wooden bed frame in Lauren's suite seems to swallow their mattress. Across the room, a pair of thick, velvet curtains are parted open so they can enjoy the Eiffel Tower's soft white lights in the distance.

She catches the delicious spicy leather scent from his shampooed hair as he rolls over to face her. His playful gaze makes her pulse race. Absence may make the heart grow fonder but for her it heightens the senses. Everything he's doing feels like the first time he did it to her.

"We have…what…about eighteen hours together until my curtain call?" she asks.

"Plenty of time before your next Paris show." His lips slowly brush across her cheek, then down and up her throat until finally pressing against her mouth. *God, eighteen hours are going to fly.*

"Mmmm…you sure didn't seem like you had plenty of time when we walked in this suite," she says.

"As soon as that door closed and we were alone, I wanted to make every second count." His teasing fingers dig into her stomach.

She squirms from his tickling touch. "Yeah, but the floor? You couldn't even push me over to the couch? And then, the shower?" She tries to kiss him again but his proud smile is too wide for her smiling lips to cover.

"Can you blame me?" His index finger gently traces her lips. "I haven't seen you in two weeks. I thought about you the whole, long flight here. Then I had to sit and watch you bend and squat in front of me on the stage. I was ready to get you alone."

She gently nips at his tracing finger. "Just so you know, I only bend and squat when you are in the audience."

He gives her a squeeze. "I would hope so."

She lies back on his chest. "So, what song was I singing when you got to the concert?"

"You were doing *Closer.*"

She rolls her eyes. "That explains why I didn't see you. You know I can't look at the audience when I sing that song. Not since…"

He squeezes her. "Baby, I know."

She shakes her head, thinking about that creepy fan with his hands down his pants during their Dallas concert. Her shock had made her forget the words to *Closer* in the middle of the song, an embarrassment she, and some of her critics, has never forgotten.

"We made good time," Andy says. "Ryan and I got to the arena pretty fast after we landed."

"I'm so glad you travel with Ryan now. I feel better knowing he is there to help you."

"Ryan helps a lot. He found Shane right after we got there. Shane was holding my seat."

"Shane is so helpful. I saw the empty chair next to him but I was trying not to look his way until you got there. Did you see who was on Shane's other side?"

"Yeah, Bruce Sanders. I don't blame you for not wanting to look at him. He's a shifty-looking dude."

She exhales an exasperated breath. "Bruce creeps me out. He's been to almost all of our shows. Shane, Johnny and Frank know I don't like him. They do a good job keeping him away from me."

"He's friendly to me; I speak his language. I work with investors like him every day."

"Johnny thinks Bruce wants to buy Platinum Plate. But Platinum Plate is totally Shane's company since Robert died. I don't think Shane wants to sell."

"Sometimes what you want means nothing when it comes to a hostile takeover," Andy says, his fingers untangling Lauren's wet hair.

"Either way, I don't like him around. I really don't like anyone around but you."

"I know, baby. It won't be long and this investment project will be wrapped up and I'll be with you for the rest of the tour. Next week I have meetings in New York City and guess where I'm staying? I booked the penthouse at The Burberry!"

"Really? Love it! I wish I could be there with you…sharing that balcony. The suite where we had our first kiss!"

Andy's arms feel warmer than their blanket. "Oh I remember that night, very well."

They lie still, both of them remembering those early days. Back then, Lauren struggled with the decision to end her marriage to Cory while Andy struggled to confess his love for Lauren. It all seems so far behind them now.

"You'll be having more fun than me." She pouts. "We're definitely in the grinding phase of this tour."

"I know Max used to keep things fun."

"He was the only person I could hang with! Lynette and Lesley are always too busy with the publicity stuff and Davis doesn't even run with me anymore. You've got Johnny and Amie plus Doug and Ashley doing everything together. The sister bond between Amie and Ashley is impossible for me to cut through. Then Michael might as well wear *I'm Mr. Negative Man* t-shirts because all he does is get snarky. Michael thinks someone fooled with the stairs, making Max fall. And he thinks it's tied to my shooting and Robert's death."

"How could that be? No way are they related."

"That's what I keep telling him! He's so negative, he's worse than Oliver. And Oliver? He's got a whole other problem…"

"What's wrong with Oliver?"

She rolls to face him, blinking heavily as the long day and exhausting concert catch up to her. Sadness weighs her eyes even more.

"He drinks. A lot. He looks and acts like regular, annoying Oliver when he's sober, but there have been a couple of functions he's missed because he's been drunk. Something is wrong: stress from this tour or maybe something with his wife Mary."

"Has Mary come to any shows?"

"I haven't seen her. I mean, how many times in my life have I seen her? The few times I have, she's nice but rarely talks. There must be some problem he's hiding. It's like he has no purpose other than to nurse a bottle of bourbon."

"Is he drunk during concerts?"

"One time, in Brussels. Davis chewed him out and it hasn't happened since. Now, Oliver just drinks behind closed doors. I think that's worse."

"None of you have ever fallen into the rock star life of drugs and alcohol."

"It's sad for me to watch," she says, looking away. "I don't want to slide down a slope because I have no purpose."

"No, baby, that won't happen to you," he says, lifting her chin so her eyes can meet his again.

"How do you know? I don't want to talk to people I don't know. I keep backing out of the meet-and-greets with fans and the media that Lynette arranges. I'm scared to not wear sunglasses on stage because I can't even look people in the eyes anymore."

Andy softly strokes her cheeks, calming her. "But you're safe now; you can do those things and feel safe."

Safe? She only feels it now, here, with him. Why can't she wrap herself in the comfort of Andy's touch all the time?

"I still don't go anywhere without Frank. He's given me all this training, an app on my phone for emergencies, plus codes and distress gestures to remember, and all of it makes me nervous. Backstage the other night, I screamed when Doug sneezed! I thought it was a gunshot! It was so embarrassing."

"Are you physically feeling okay?"

"I'm so tired all the time. I'd rather sleep all day than go see any sights. That's just not the person I used to be. I've changed."

"Maybe they did this tour too soon."

"Maybe we shouldn't have toured at all. Why can't Johnny, Oliver, Michael, Doug and I just go into a studio, write music we love, record great songs for people to enjoy and leave it at that?"

"Sounds like you want to go back in time as an unknown, before Plebeian was revealed."

She barely remembers her life before Plebeian was revealed.

"I'd go back to the beginning, except add you from the start," she says, rolling on top of him. Her damp hair falls into his face, her lips teasingly hover above his. She'd like nothing more than to devour his lips right now, but first she needs something only he can offer: reassurance. "You really think I'm safe? All this is unrelated bad luck?"

Andy moves her dangling hair from his cheek and nods. "You are safe. It's just a bunch of bad luck. No one is out to get you, except me." He grabs her ass.

That makes her want to change the subject. Enough gossip; it's time to play with her husband.

She gently rubs her nose over Andy's face, pulling back for the sight of his hazelnut-olive eyes, thin nose and those lips she could kiss for hours. Her body warms with pleasure just looking at him, the same way she did back in high school when he passed her in the hall. Every day, she feels like the lucky one to finally have him now.

"You are an amazing husband. Thank you for listening."

"Thank you for taking a chance and loving me."

Strands of his straight, brown hair move with the slow touch of her fingers; her mind fills with happy and not-so-happy memories. When they were dating and Andy broke up with her, his week-long drunken romp with another woman was one of the lowest lows of her life. But it was a complicated time. A car accident had triggered fears from his abusive childhood and he made bad choices to deal with his pain. Her nagging didn't help their problem either. But that episode is behind them. In the end, she has no regrets. He's her husband now. He's her everything.

"Andy, I love you with everything I have."

He squeezes her rear. "Show me everything you have."

She softly bites his smiling lips and gives him what he wants.

[THREE]

Rumblings of early morning thunder rattle the car window. Lauren presses her droopy face against the vibrating glass anyway. Her stare is just as sad as the raindrops streaking down the glass. Did it have to be a dreary, rainy day when Andy left?

Their driver returns her and Frank to their Madrid hotel, completing their morning trip to drop off Andy and Ryan at the airport.

"Want to get some breakfast before you go up to your room?" Frank asks, opening her car door.

"Sweet of you to ask," she says. "I just want to bury my face in my pillow and try to forget Andy's gone."

"He'll be back by the time we reach Vienna."

"I know; two weeks." Her head slumps. "I just wish it was sooner."

They walk through the revolving glass doors of Hotel Savarana, where Plebeian arrived late last night after their Barcelona show. Tonight will be the first of two concerts in Madrid. No fans have camped outside the hotel yet and only a few guests are wandering around the lobby in this early morning hour. Soft Spanish music and the splashing indoor water fountain are the only sounds.

"Looks like I'm not the only one up this early," Lauren says, pointing to a bistro table outside the lobby café. Doug sits alone, rubbing a coffee cup. She turns to Frank. "It's so rare to see him without Ashley attached to his hip. Give me a minute."

Frank does what Frank does best: disappears within easy reach of Lauren.

"Anyone sitting here?" Lauren asks Doug.

His eyes widen, his smile warm. "You up early too?"

"Just took Andy to the airport. Not a good day so far," she says, taking a seat.

"Not a good day for me, either," he says, staring back down at his orange ceramic cup.

How unusual: a chat with Doug? He's the refreshing silence among the noisy voices and loud sounds of their band. But since he's been dating his bubbly girlfriend Ashley, he does seem to talk more often. Usually in rare, little blurts of conversation.

"What has you up so early?" Lauren asks.

He shifts in his chair, his eyes darting around the lobby for anyone who might overhear.

"Can I ask you something?"

"Ask away."

"Do you think what Michael's been saying is right?"

"You mean his crazy theory about Robert Burgess's death and Max's accident?"

"Yeah, and your shooting. Do you think something bigger is happening here?"

"No way, Doug. Look, I had some suspicions but Andy helped me talk it out. This is all just bad luck."

"Even what happened with Johnny's guitars last night?"

Her eyes roll. "Refretting emergencies can happen on tours. If the guitars weren't packed right after the last show, the frets could have popped out."

"The *same* frets? On *all* of Johnny's guitars?"

"I don't think anyone messed with his guitars. Besides, Trent is the best production manager of any band in the world. His techs fixed it and the show started on time. No one got hurt."

Doug smiles, still rubbing his coffee cup.

She watches his constant, nervous rubbing. Why would a drummer be having a bad day worried about guitar frets? "Is this why you're up so early?"

He lowers his eyes.

"I was wondering about something else," he says. "It's about you… and Cory."

She leans back. How the heck is this conversation now swinging towards her ex-husband? "Me and Cory?"

"Yeah. I wanted to ask you something."

"Well, not much in my life is a secret anymore. Go ahead."

"I know you guys met in college after you and Johnny broke up. Then you and Cory got married right away. But was that a good idea?"

She quickly sifts through his loaded question. Obviously it wasn't a good idea to get married right away because she and Cory are now divorced. But someone who asks an obvious question isn't looking for the obvious answer.

"Good idea? I don't think Cory and I were meant to be but there was some good that came from our marriage."

"Yeah, Lee and Aiden turned out great," Doug says. "You had Lee right after you got married, right?"

What the hell?

"We did. It's no secret to those who knew us at the time. I was pregnant right before Cory and I got married. That moved things along…maybe too fast."

Doug smiles, looking again at the safety of his coffee cup.

Talking marriage and babies with Doug? What a weird, shifty little conversation.

He licks his lips and looks up. "I got Ashley pregnant."

"Oh, wow," she says, leaning closer. Mom-mode kicks in. "You know you didn't do this by yourself."

"It feels like I did," he says. "I think I'm going to ask her to marry me now."

"A baby is an incredible thing. So is marriage."

"What do you think I should do?"

She's so glad he asked. "If you were trying to foresee your future by asking me about my past, I'd suggest you wait a bit before you get married."

"But you were always pushing Johnny to marry Amie."

"That was different. Johnny started dating Amie right after he and I broke up. They've been together for years. I knew he loved Amie and wanted to get married but he was always too chicken to ask. Their situation was different than yours."

Across the quiet lobby, the elevator dings. The doors open and Johnny appears. His wavy black hair is in order this morning and a button-down olive shirt is tucked into his faded jeans. He spots Doug and Lauren and heads their way.

Lauren whispers, "I'm assuming Ashley told Amie who told Johnny?"

"These sisters don't keep any secrets, so yeah, Johnny knows. I haven't told anyone else yet."

Lauren smiles. Usually a perky smile hides her stress but now she's hoping a warm smile shares her compassion. It's hard for her to watch someone struggle. If only there was more she could do to help. "Listen, if you need someone to talk to, I'm here."

Doug nods.

Johnny arrives, plopping a folded Spanish newspaper on the table.

"Don't shoot the messenger," he tells Doug. "The girls want to leave soon and are wondering if you're ready."

"Awww…" Lauren says, smirking. "Another day of holding Amie and Ashley's shopping bags?"

Johnny flings her a disgusted look. "It's a family obligation."

"Shopping? A family obligation? Hey, speaking of family, I'm glad I have the two of you right now. The three of us have a little problem."

Doug stiffens.

"Relax," she says. "It's *my* family causing the problem."

Johnny straddles a bistro chair. "This ought to be good."

"Andy brought some disturbing news from home," she says, trying to act serious. "Evidently, in our absence, our home studio has been overtaken by teenagers."

"Ha! Is Lee finally playing guitar like I taught him?" Johnny asks.

"Oh, he's playing like you taught him, with the goal of replacing you. And we have Aiden on drums; the little monster you created, Doug. And Brittney is doing the vocals. My boys and Andy's daughter have formed a band."

"Little mini us," Doug says, amused.

"Ready for their name? The LAB band. Get it? Lee, Aiden, Brittney: LAB." Lauren laughs.

"That's too stupid a name to keep," Johnny says.

"Oh, it's staying. Lee wants their first album to be called "Chocolate Lab" and Aiden wants their first single to be "Ruff Life.""

"None of that can happen. Ever," Johnny says. "Isn't Lee getting ready to go off to college in a week or so anyway?"

"He'll just be across town, close enough that they'll still practice on Sunday nights."

"Then every Sunday, Andy needs to cut off the power to the studio," Johnny says.

Another ding of an arriving elevator draws their attention. Out step Shane and Bruce Sanders. Shane's appearance never disappoints. Today he's wearing crisp jeans, a collared blue shirt and quarter-zip blue sweater. Bruce looks like a high-stakes Vegas player with slicked-back hair, casual slacks and summer-weight tweed sport coat. They head Lauren's way.

Lauren leans closer to Johnny and Doug. "Don't tell Shane about The LAB band. He'd probably sign them!"

"I'm outta here," Doug says, getting up. "See you up in the room, Johnny. I'd rather spend the day shopping than one minute yakking with Bruce."

Johnny's eyes lock with Lauren's.

"No one wants to spend time with Bruce Sanders, except Shane," Johnny says.

"Well that's what record execs like Shane have to do, hang with all sorts of creepy people to keep everyone happy. Just keep me away from…"

"Lauren!" Bruce says, extending his arms for an embrace.

She launches a tepid smile and remains seated. "Good morning, Bruce. You're up early. Didn't you host a big party again last night?"

"We missed you, sweetheart," he says, rubbing her shoulders. "You should have come! Oliver was there and once again was the hit of the evening. Is Andy gone now?"

Her insides tighten. Does he think since her husband's gone she'll party with him now?

"It looks like we're interrupting your coffee," Shane says with a perfectly timed distraction, pointing to the orange coffee cup that neither Johnny nor Lauren was drinking from.

"Yeah, we've been down here all morning working on the next hit single," Johnny says.

"Perfect!" Bruce says, his domineering voice filling the quiet lobby. "By the time I get Shane here to let me invest in you, we'll take that single right to the top!"

Lauren looks at Johnny. This idiot has no idea what he's talking about.

"Or, you could just stick to throwing fabulous parties," she says.

Bruce leans down, his strong hands tightening his grip on her shoulders. "My parties can't be fabulous without you, honey." He grips tighter. "Come up to my suite tonight after the concert. Everyone will want to meet you!"

Her shiver runs head to toe.

As Bruce stands, Johnny rises to get in his face. "We don't roll like that."

Shane steps in to separate them. "Hey, we've got a group touring the Prado Museum and then having lunch. Would you and Lauren like to join us?"

Thoughts of a meal with Bruce rouse a gas bubble from Lauren's stomach.

"Oh, wish I could," she tells Shane, reaching for his hand. "But I've made plans." Her hot plans involve a pillow and a day of sleep. Alone.

She's reassured by Shane's squeeze. Thank goodness he is here to buffer Bruce.

Bruce turns to greet their tour group now arriving in the lobby. Lauren tugs Shane closer.

"How can you stand that guy?" she whispers.

"Bruce could help me a lot with my plan to open a movie production studio," Shane whispers back. "It's just business."

Lauren drops his hand. "You're all business, Shane."

"Have to be right now, with Plebeian on tour."

"Are we always dollar signs to you?" she says, smiling.

"Sure, but you know you mean more to me than that."

"I know, I know; I'm your favorite dollar sign."

"Since the beginning."

"Yeah, about that…sorry I haven't had any drama in my life since I was shot and left for dead in a steakhouse parking lot. I know my drama drives record sales."

"Don't joke about that, Lauren. You almost died. No amount of money could have brought you back."

The sudden, saddened look in Shane's brown eyes tell her he's serious. He really does care more about her than the money she brings.

Johnny sits down. "By the way Shane, happy birthday."

"Thanks, pal."

"Whoa! I didn't know. Happy birthday! How old are you anyway?" Lauren asks.

"Ancient. Thirty-seven," Shane says.

"Please! You're only a few years younger than us. What do you want for your birthday?" she asks.

"Oh, I know what I want," Shane says. "I just have to wait for it to arrive."

"You? Wait?" she asks. "You have the money to get anything you want!"

"And I'll get what I want, someday," Shane says, his eyes now distracted by something in the café. "Looks like that lady over there is totally going to…"

Loud crashing fills the lobby.

Lauren jumps from her chair, lurching away from the sound. Shane catches her as Johnny jumps up and Frank bolts to her side. Lauren's heart pounds and her cheeks feel flushed. She clenches Shane's arms, looking back to the cafe. Panic blurs her eyes as she tries to see what just happened.

"Just a dropped tray," Frank says.

She nods, relaxing her grip on Shane's tight arms. *Calm down. Coffee cups are not trying to kill you. Breathe.* With her eyes on the floor, she slinks back to her seat.

Shane exchanges concerned glances with Johnny, who slowly sits back down.

"I'm watching the lobby," Frank says. "I'm always watching."

She nods, breathing deep to slow her racing heart. "I know," she mumbles. "Thank you, Frank." She places her hand on the table, fingers flat, and looks at him.

Frank sees her hand, nods and moves away.

She's not in distress now. If she was, her hand would be fisted, like he taught her. One of the many signals she has learned.

"You okay?" Shane whispers.

"I'm fine, thanks." She points across the lobby to change subjects. "Oh boy, here comes your date."

Watching Bruce swagger back to their table is making her nauseous again and tempting her to fist both hands.

"Ready, Shane?" Bruce asks.

"All set," Shane says, smiling. Lauren taps his hand in a friendly smack and he gives Johnny a departing fist bump. "See you guys later."

Johnny and Lauren sit alone, watching Shane's group leave. Splashes from the fountain and broken coffee cup pieces being swept into dustpans are now the only sounds in the lobby.

Lauren wants to talk about anything but her reaction to spilled coffee.

"So, last night's show. Everything seemed okay after the tech fixed your guitars, right?" she asks.

"Sure, they sounded fine," Johnny says. "Now I need to find out who fucked with them in the first place."

"The frets could have popped out during transport. You know that."

His look scolds. "Not every second and fourth fret, on every guitar. Maybe Michael is right. Maybe bad luck started for us the day you were shot."

"Oh, so this is all my fault now?" she says, stiffening.

"No. But our bad luck did begin as soon as you were shot. We've toured in the past and never had a problem."

"What? Andy and I were almost killed by a drunk driver after the show in Dallas! I'd say that was a problem."

Johnny nods. "Yeah, come to think of it, all the bad luck does happen around you." He smiles like he's joking, but Lauren's not sure. Is *she* really the reason bad things keep happening? Can't be; she has nothing to do with guitars or staircases! But right now she doesn't have the confidence to debate him. She can't even keep her cool when coffee cups fall.

She'd rather switch the subject. Again.

"So, Doug's news…that's something, huh?"

Johnny leans closer. "Did he tell you he's thinking about asking Ashley to marry him?"

"He did. He was asking me about my past, I think as some way to gauge his decision. I told him I'm no role model."

"If we could all go back to our twenties, we'd probably do most things differently."

Her head tilts. *Really?* They dated when they were in their early twenties! She would have married Johnny if he had asked. Does he want a mulligan on one or both of those?

"So, how is Amie dealing with the news that her younger sister is pregnant?" she asks.

He looks down, rotating the folded newspaper to face him.

"Are you avoiding my question by pretending you can read Spanish?"

He smiles. "No, I was just trying to think of the best words."

"Hey, if this is too personal, you don't have to tell me," she says.

"Please. You and I have been through way too much. Amie is happy for Ashley and Doug. She's decided she'd rather be an aunt than a mom. We are not going to have children."

Her head jerks back. "Whoa. She decided? Are you okay with that?"

Johnny's eyes search the lobby, his glazed stare searching for distractions. "I had a child. I just didn't get to raise her."

Anna. Just thinking about Anna's death blurs Lauren's eyes. Johnny only got to hold Anna for less than an hour before she died. And worse, Amie knew about Anna's condition for months and never told Johnny, never gave him the chance to prepare. It's not fair that he never got a lifetime to love her.

His weathered fingers rub the corners of the newspaper. "If I go through life and Anna's the only child I ever have, I'm okay with that."

Bullshit. He's saying the company line for his wife. But, it's hard not to admire a guy who puts his needs aside to support his spouse. "You're a special kind of guy, Johnny Fulton."

And off his fingers go, pulling through his wavy black hair. Lauren's always loved watching him do that.

More early-rising guests are now wandering around the hotel lobby. It won't be long until someone recognizes them and approaches for photos or autographs. And if someone takes photos of the two of them alone, the next round of *Johnny and Lauren are getting back together* rumors could ignite. Luckily, the arriving elevator has brought them company.

Oliver stumbles out, wearing wrinkled jeans and a crooked baseball cap. He zigzags their way.

Lauren squints to get a better look at his t-shirt. The exposed back tag confirms it: his shirt is inside out. At least his shoes match. "Wow, you look…pretty awful."

"There's a good chance I feel awful too." His bony finger points to the café. "Muffin and milk."

"Muffin and milk?"

Johnny nods. "That's Oliver's standard hangover remedy."

"They can bring muffins and milk to your room, you know. Room service?" She hates to push a man when he's down but when it comes to Oliver, she'll give a gentle nudge.

"I have to pick my muffin," Oliver mumbles. He slithers inside the café to place his order. Thank goodness no paparazzi are here to take a picture of *that*.

"Well, this has been the strangest walk into a hotel lobby that I've ever had," Lauren says, looking over her shoulder to see where Frank has been hiding. He emerges, standing next to a five-foot potted plant.

"I like to see Frank watching you so closely," Johnny says.

"See? No need for you to worry about me because Frank is," she says, smiling. Johnny's always kept one watchful eye on every man she's dated and the other eye on her to make sure she's okay. *Sweet Captain Control.* But oddly, since her shooting he doesn't ask if she's okay as much as he used to. He's calmed down with her. Maybe since he married Amie, she told him to.

"I've gotta go shopping," Johnny says, lowering his head.

"I've gotta go sleep," she says. "See you tonight. Wear black."

"Bring your voice," he says, standing. A mischievous smile stretches across his face.

Of course you're going to…

He blows her a kiss.

Knew it! They part ways, Lauren smiling as she walks with Frank up to her room.

The simple walk into the hotel lobby has created quite a to-do list for Lauren. She needs to get a baby gift for Doug and Ashley. She should get a birthday gift for Shane. She'll need antacids to calm her stomach the next time she sees Bruce, and she should probably carry a can of mace. She wonders if someone should keep an eye on Oliver and his drinking, now that he's wearing his clothes inside out.

She also needs to remember that sounds of everyday life are not bullets meant to kill. Andy is right: no one is out to get her. No one is out to get this band either. Instead of thinking she causes the bad luck, maybe she can put everyone's worries to rest and figure out why bad luck keeps happening. Plebeian is not in danger. Maybe she can prove it.

But the action item on top of her list is the same one she walked in with: figuring out how she can see Andy sooner than two weeks.

[FOUR]

The rain in Spain has followed Plebeian to Portugal. And that's a problem.

Davis talks on the phone with their tour promoter about flooding in the Lisbon venue. He paces the floor in his preppy blue boat shoes, his eyes in a serious squint. His free hand keeps swatting popcorn from his hair.

"Quit throwing crap at him—this is serious," Johnny whispers to Oliver, sitting in the living room of Davis's suite.

Oliver shoves a handful of popcorn in his mouth, chewing with his mouth open. With a devious smile, he reaches back inside the popcorn bag, pulling out one kernel. He flicks it into Michael's face.

"Shhh! I'm trying to hear what Davis is saying," Michael says.

"I'm pretty sure that popcorn was quiet," Oliver says.

Davis turns to face them, still talking. "Okay, we'll work on the rescheduled date. I'll let them know." He hangs up. "The Lisbon arena is still flooded. Looks like you get the night off."

"Voodoo tour strikes again! Open the bar!" Oliver says, peeling cellophane from a cigar.

Davis turns to Shane. "All of this massive rain. The stage was fine but they couldn't clear the floodwater from the floor, so it's not safe for fans."

"Actually, this delay is great news," Johnny says to Davis. "Now you have time to chat with our projectionist and find out why some of our damn videos didn't work again last night."

"Give it up, Johnny," Michael says. "Bad luck is the mascot of this tour."

"It was a faulty cable that caused intermittent failure," Lauren says. "I asked him last night what went wrong."

"Oh great," Oliver says. "Now our lead singer is the new technical director."

"No, I'm the lead singer and the new logical director because apparently I'm the only one who thinks logically."

"Well, Mrs. Logical Director," Oliver says, chewing the end of his cigar, "the busted cable only confirms that bad luck is still our mascot."

Her teeth grind. Oliver looks like a horse chewing cud with that cigar hanging out of his mouth. Michael has become an oversized worry-wart. Davis should be at the helm of a sailboat with those damn boat shoes he always wears. Johnny's irritation is getting annoying. And is Doug even in this room?

Oliver pulls the wet cigar from his mouth. "Voodoo tour keeps dishing out the bad luck and that's fine by me. Now we have a vacation. No show tonight, then we head to Rome tomorrow, where we have two days off anyway."

What a great chance to get away from these guys. She leans closer to Frank. "It looks like I would have plenty of time. Should I go?"

"I've got a charter flight company on standby since Cory has the plane with the boys in Hawaii. They only need a two-hour notice, and then we can head to New York City to surprise Andy," Frank says. "If we leave by six p.m. we can be there a little after ten p.m. with time zone changes."

"Let's go! I'd have a two-day visit with Andy before the first Rome show!"

"Are you taking off?" Shane asks, sitting next to Lauren on the sofa.

"Yeah…I'll be taking off my clothes with Andy in just a few hours," she says, smiling, already lost in a daydream about how she'll surprise him.

Shane's eyes widen.

"Oh geez, I'm sorry, Shane. That was totally inappropriate for me to say that."

"Have fun," he says. "Wish it was me."

"Shane! Now you sound as creepy as Bruce!"

"No! I meant me taking off, time off." He laughs. "Okay, this conversation is over."

Lauren taps his leg. "I'll see you in Rome."

* * *

The city lights roll out their nightly welcome while cab horns blare with irritation that anyone is here. Lauren takes in the sights and sounds of New York City as her driver approaches The Burberry hotel. In minutes she'll see Andy's surprised face and seconds later be wrinkling the sheets with him in the penthouse suite. It was totally worth her time to get away from all the world tour drama, even if her time with Andy will be squeezed in between his business meetings.

The doorman welcomes Lauren with a warm smile.

"Good evening, Mrs. Hayden!" he says. "I didn't realize you were staying with Mr. Hayden this trip."

"He doesn't know I'm staying with him either!" Lauren says, walking into the familiar, neoclassical hotel. "I had an impromptu break from our tour and wanted to see my favorite guy."

She and Frank reach the penthouse floor and head straight to Ryan's room.

"Hey there," Ryan says, welcoming them. What a good idea it had been to assign Ryan to Andy. Lauren's fans have become Andy's fans since he saved her life after the shooting, and Andy was constantly being asked for autographs or photos wherever he went. Ryan helps with logistics and security whenever Andy travels.

"You didn't spill the beans, did you?" Lauren asks.

"He doesn't know. He's going to be so excited!" Ryan says.

"Well, Andy always surprises me with the sweetest things, like the roses he sends to every hotel I've been at on tour. It's time for me to have a nice surprise for him." The pink, satin-and-lace teddy in her suitcase is one of those surprises.

"We got back from dinner about an hour ago." Ryan hands her the extra key card. "He mentioned he wasn't feeling well, so he may already be asleep."

"Wonder if it was something he ate? Well, I wasn't planning to walk in and scare him. I'm gonna call first. Then surprise him by being right outside the door."

"We're just down the hall in case you need us," Frank says. "Call in the morning if you want to go anywhere."

"Thanks, but don't wake up early expecting us to call." She adds a wink. "You too, Ryan. You guys can get some much deserved rest."

She heads down the hall towards the penthouse door. Bright wall sconces light her path while Frank watches her from the doorway of his room. Her call to Andy goes to his voicemail as she and her suitcase wait outside the door. So much for calling first; he must already be asleep. She tries calling again, at the same time using her key card to open the door and giving a goodbye nod to Frank.

"Andy?" she whispers, stepping inside.

The penthouse is dark, except for the moonlight filtering through open curtains and the soft glow from Andy's vibrating phone on the coffee table. His caller ID says, "My Lover."

Oh my God, that's so cute!

She ends the call and hears rustling from the bedroom. *Crap— what now?* She doesn't want to scare him if he's sleeping!

She steps closer to the bedroom, standing now in the middle of the living room. The spot where they shared their first kiss! That summer night so long ago was filled with confessions and hints about their future as a couple. They made delicious martinis, danced barefoot and then he surprised her with the kiss that started it all.

She smiles and looks down at her feet.

There's a pair of women's shoes by the couch.

Her heart pounds.

She looks towards the bedroom. On the floor, it looks like a skirt; maybe a dress?

Oh my God, she's in the wrong room!

Panic moves her body backwards.

Logic makes her stop.

This is the right room. Andy's phone is on the coffee table and her key opened the door.

Her hands shake. Her chest pounds.

Something isn't right; this can't be right.

Bones in her feet creak with every uneasy step she takes towards the bedroom. She stops once she has a clear view of the bed.

Under the sheets, a woman sits atop a man, rising with a giggle. The white sheet slides off her body, the porcelain skin of her bare back visible to Lauren in the moonlit room. The woman grinds her hips down on the man.

His sounds, his groans. The man is Andy.

Horror freezes Lauren and her breath leaves her. Her voice that sings to millions suddenly cannot utter a sound.

Panicked, one-word fragments pulse in her brain.

Andy?

No.

No!

Run!

Stay?

Help!

Frank.

She looks down to her phone, quivering in her violently shaking hand.

Frank trained her for emergencies. But he never trained her for this.

Help!

Do it!
Red app.
Hit.
Keypad.
1216
Star.

Her posture melts and her shoulders fall. Her legs loosen, ready to cave. She stands four feet from the end of the bed, her eyes burning as she watches the end of her marriage.

"Andy?" she whispers, her voice soft and frightened in disbelief.

The door bursts open, the metal doorknob crashing into drywall.

"Lauren?" Ryan screams, but Frank has already reached her.

She hasn't moved, still staring in shock at her cheating husband.

The woman scrambles off Andy, ripping off the top sheet as she runs to the other side of the bed for her clothes.

"Lauren?" Andy slurs, trying to lift his head.

"Who the hell are you?" Ryan yells, blocking the woman's exit. Her clothes are clutched in one hand, the white sheet bunched in the other to cover her naked body. She reaches for her purse by the wet bar but Ryan grabs it first. Before he can grab her, she runs out the door.

"Lauren? Oh my gawd! How'd you get over there, baby?" Andy slurs, grabbing the side of the bed, struggling to sit up.

Frank's arms surround Lauren as she watches her naked, drunk husband fall out of bed.

Ryan rushes to Andy, trying to lift him off the floor.

"Why are the people here?" Andy slurs from the carpet.

Warm saliva fills Lauren's mouth, tempting her to spit. Instead, she swallows hard. "You said you'd never do this again," she whispers. "You promised I would be the last."

Ryan pushes Andy to sit upright, still struggling to lift him up. Andy's glassy eyes can't seem to focus on anything as his head wobbles loosely. His body teeters to the right and he falls to the floor again.

"Get me out of here," she says.

"Secure everything, Ryan—*everything!*" Frank yells.

* * *

Her body sits rigid in a catatonic state. Lauren can't even feel the soft leather seat of her own Chevy Tahoe.

The traffic lights blur as her driver Bill speeds through the open roads of Tampa in the early morning hour. He could be running red lights for all she knows. She wouldn't care if he did.

Bill safely pulls under the portico of her home.

"Thanks again, Bill, for coming in the middle of the night like this," Frank says. He turns to Lauren. "You sure you want him to wait? You really want to drive back to the airport and fly back to Europe tonight?"

She snaps back to the present, nodding. "This will only take a minute," she whispers.

Frank opens the front door; the ten-foot, glass door dwarfs her slouched body. She steps inside, feeling as empty as a shadow. Her beautiful home is dark and quiet, cold even on such a warm summer night. The love that once filled the house is as good as dead. Her shadow moves through the house like an eerie houseguest, Frank an arm's length behind her.

She heads straight to the kitchen.

Padded barstools are lined in orderly fashion behind one of the kitchen islands; empty placemats lie in front of each. An empty fruit bowl sits lonely on the counter; the kids haven't been home for awhile now. The soft glow from a night light near the sink guides her.

Lauren stops at a utensil drawer and slowly opens it. Her fingers glide over the metal loops of a whisk and move over the sanded surface of a wooden spoon. The sharp, jagged teeth of a can opener rub the side of her finger as she nudges a spatula aside. There it is.

She snatches the six-inch paring knife.

Frank stiffens and moves closer.

Clutching the knife, she spins to the left, away from the drawer, stepping out of the kitchen, back to the foyer and up the stairs.

Frank follows her.

The doors of her bedroom creak as she pushes them open, stepping into her place of peace, her refuge, the sacred domain where she's free to unleash her passion. Now, she feels unwelcome here. Right now, nothing feels the same.

Her steps are soft, like the moon's light straining through the open curtains. Frank follows so closely his shadow has merged with hers.

There are no tears; her face is blank. Numb, raw, stripped as naked as the woman she saw on top of her husband.

She moves to the side of the bed, letting her fingers gently trail across the comforter's soft sateen fabric. Her skin had been cushioned by its softness so many times when Andy would make love to her on it and under it.

But her issue is not with this comforter.

She yanks her hand back. Her other hand rises, squeezing the knife.

Vengeance drives the knife down, the blade piercing the soft, gray fabric of the little, square H pillow.

She plunges again and again, slicing into the gift from Andy that he had embroidered with the initial of their last name. Now the pillow that symbolized their love is a tragic, helpless victim.

She stabs harder, faster. White foam filling silently explodes over the bed as she chops and gouges; Frank stands stoic behind her.

Faster. Deeper. Harder.

Suddenly she stops.

Her chest heaves with angry breaths as she surveys the damage.

Slowly, she tilts her head, nodding.

"He's lucky he wasn't lying here," she whispers.

She gently lays the knife on the exposed pillow stuffing, slices of dead gray fabric littering the white comforter.

"Let's go."

[FIVE]

Tourists scurry like busy ants through the streets of Rome on this warm, summer evening. Lauren and Frank sit in silence as their driver pulls up to the entrance of Plebeian's hotel.

"Did you just land and turn right around or something?" Davis asks, opening Lauren's car door.

She ignores him and marches into the lobby.

"Just show us where her room is," Frank calmly says.

"Sure," Davis says, catching up to Lauren with energetic steps. "You're in the same clothes you wore when you left yesterday! You okay?"

"Davis, the room," Frank says. "This is a new hotel to us. Show us her room."

Davis leads them across the lobby to the elevators.

"Who is around now?" she mutters as they step into the elevator.

"Most everyone is gone. Johnny, Doug and the sisters took a train to Venice and have been gone since yesterday. Today, Michael went to tour some museums. Oliver just got back from dinner with Shane and Bruce," Davis says.

They arrive on the eighth floor.

"All our suites are on this floor," Davis says, handing a room key to Frank. "You're right here, 8162."

Frank stops to insert the key card.

"Which suite is Bruce's?" she asks.

Frank freezes.

"Um, down that way, 8168," Davis says. "You don't want to go there, do…"

She's already walked away.

She stands outside 8168, and knocks.

Bruce opens the door. "Lauren!" he says. "You're back!"

His slicked-back hair looks as wretched as usual. Spending one minute with him is one minute too long. But he has something she needs. "You throw parties; you must have good alcohol."

"Of course! Join us for an after-dinner drink."

The mahogany-paneled suite is dimly lit. Oliver stands behind a small corner bar. Shane is on the other side of the room. Davis and Frank cautiously follow Lauren inside.

She heads straight for the bar.

"You're back early," Bruce says.

"My plans changed." She pushes Oliver out of the way to survey her options.

But Oliver steps back towards her, leaning closer with focused, intense eyes. "Facts, Lauren," he whispers. "You need to listen to the facts."

Her eyebrows screw tight. *What the hell is he talking about? And why is he whispering?*

"Bourbon your dessert tonight, Oliver?" she whispers back.

"I'm not drinking tonight and neither should you," he says, hand on her arm.

She leans closer, inches from his face. "Who the hell are you to stop me?"

"There's a lot going on that you don't know."

She shakes his hand off her arm. *No, Oliver. You have no idea what is going on. And why are you whispering!?*

She finds her vice: tequila. She pours a shot, forgets the salt, tosses it back, bites a wedge of lime, then throws the bitten lime into Davis's shocked face.

"Good stuff, Bruce," she hollers, tipping the bottle to pour another. Oliver grabs the bottle. "Lauren, listen."

She tugs the bottle out of his bony hand and pours. Glass up, tosses it back, bites a lime, throws it at Davis.

"I remember this from my college sorority days!" she says. "I have a toast for you, my good friend Oliver." Before she says the words she pours another shot. Glass up, tosses it back, bites a lime, throws it at Davis. She pours another.

"Okay, for you, Oliver!" She raises her shot glass and looks into Oliver's wide eyes. "Here's to you, here's to me, best of friends we'll always be, if by chance we disagree, fuck you—here's to me!"

Glass up, tosses it back, bites a lime, throws it at Davis.

"Aw, are there no other women up here but me?" she asks, looking around the suite. Frank stands at the edge of the bar, exchanging glances with Bruce, Shane and Davis.

"No, hon'," Bruce says. "Just us guys."

"Ohhh, cuz I got a toast for my ladies too." She primes the toast by first taking a shot. Glass up, tosses it back, bites a lime, throws it at Davis.

She pours another. "Okay, so here's my toast. This is for the ladies so you stupid guys should just close your stupid ears." She raises her shot glass. "Here's to the men that we love, here's to the men that love us, but the men that we love aren't the men that love us, so *to hell* with the men, *here's to us!*"

Tosses it back, bites a lime and Davis moves so she can't throw it at him. She throws it at Oliver instead.

"Stop," Oliver says, grabbing her arm.

"Get your hand off me *now.*"

"Okay, Lauren, let's go back to your suite," Davis says, reaching for her.

"*Don't touch me, Davis!*" she yells. "*No one touch me!*"

Frank steps closer.

"*Leave me alone!*" she screams to Frank, her neck veins throbbing.

A majority of the tequila she's trying to pour ends up on the counter but enough fills her glass for another shot. Glass up, toss it back.

"Oh schit! Where are the limes?" she slurs, holding up the empty lime cup.

Shane comes closer, joining her behind the bar.

"I don't see any more limes here," he calmly says, looking around. "Let's go back to your suite and look there."

His steady voice calms her. "Good plan!"

She walks with Shane's helpful arm around her waist. Frank follows.

"Stay here. I need to keep her calm," Frank tells Davis. Oliver and Bruce stand in silence.

Frank opens the door to 8162 and he, Lauren and Shane step inside.

"Look, Lauren, all your things are already here," he says, pointing to her suitcases. "This is a good time to unpack, get a good shower and some rest."

"Pfffttt," she spits in Frank's direction. "Where's the limes?"

"Let's look," Shane calmly says, walking with Lauren towards the mini-bar.

"There's, like, nothing even, like, alcohol here," she says, head tilted, looking at the barren mini-bar.

"Oh well, no limes!" Shane says.

"We can have some water," Frank says.

"Crap that, Frank!" she says. "Let's go back to Bruce's!"

"Lauren, we need to stay here," Frank says.

No Frank," she yells, pushing him.

"We have to stay here," Frank says.

"No!" she screams. "Take me back *now!*"

Shane steps between them. "Frank, I have an idea. Why don't you go see if Bruce has found more limes? I'll stay here with Lauren."

Lauren looks at Shane and nods. She likes his plan. Whatever Shane says, she likes.

Shane whispers to Frank, "Everyone seems to agitate her except me. Just come back in five minutes and tell her you forgot what you were looking for. I'll keep her calm and maybe she'll forget the whole thing."

"Lauren, are you okay if I leave to look for more limes?" Frank asks.

She's already wandered across the living room. "Ohhh shure," she says, now looking behind the drapes for limes.

Frank whispers to Shane, "She left her purse at Bruce's. I'll go get it and tell them to forget what they just saw. Keep her calm like this. I'll be back in four minutes."

Shane nods and closes the door behind Frank.

"Come, let's sit down!" Shane says, reaching for her hand. He leads her to the sofa as she playfully swings his hand behind him. He stops to face her but she runs into him.

"I don't wanna sit," she says, slowly looking up at him. A wide smile stretches across her face. "I wanna play."

She drops his hand and grabs the bottom of her shirt, yanking it up and over her head. A black satin push-up bra she intended for her husband to see is now in Shane's view. "Do you wanna play?" She tilts her head.

Shane's eyes bulge as Lauren moves closer. She reaches behind her back and unfastens her bra, hitting a lamp with it as she throws it across the room. Her bare chest pushes into him as he reaches to embrace, and steady, her.

"I'd rather bite you than limes," she purrs, pulling his head down to hers. His lips become hers as she devours him in aggressive kisses, squeezing his head and rubbing her topless body on him. Tasting Shane makes her thirst for more, her body gushing in a raging turn-on. Her mouth wants more. More!

"Lauren, you've been drinking," Shane whispers, his mouth on her ear.

"I know." She teeters backwards to give him a good view of her bare chest, and then grabs him again for more kissing. "You are one good-looking, delishious lime."

Her fingers race down his shirt, unleashing each button so her bare chest can feel his. Soon they're skin to skin, her lips pressing his hard. *More! She wants more!* And what she wants now is underneath his jeans. Her hands drop to unbutton them.

"Are you sure?" Shane breathlessly asks.

"Are you kidding?" She pushes him towards the bedroom.

Lips to lips and hands to hair they stumble closer to ecstasy. The crisp, white comforter caves when their bodies collapse on the bed. Lauren rushes to push off her jeans and help Shane out of his.

"I'm moving on," she whispers. "Make love to me, Shane."

He's already on top of her when she asks.

"Lauren," he whispers, "I have wanted you for years."

The room is spinning from the view of her drunken eyes yet she knows damn well who she is with.

Shane Mitchell. Her new lover.

Forget Andy Hayden.

[SIX]

Three soft courtesy knocks sound on the suite door, then Frank opens it with his key card.

"Your breakfast is here," he yells from the door.

"Be out in a minute!" Lauren yells from the bedroom.

Shane rolls off Lauren, panting.

"Just got that one off in time," he whispers.

She giggles. "I can't believe we did it again." She rolls on her side to face him, raising her thigh to rest on the outside of his leg. "You have blown what was left of my mind."

"You have always blown my mind." He gently moves her messy brown hair off her face. His finger traces her jaw. "You've got to be exhausted. From what you told me you saw in New York, plus so much flying in such a short time. Then very little sleep last night."

Her fingers play with his sandy brown hair, so soft she can't stop touching it. "But very little sleep with you was worth every bit of sleep lost," she says, grinning through a pounding headache. "Did that make sense?"

"Pretty coherent considering what you've just been through." His proud smile lights up the room. "Any regrets?"

Regrets? *Hell yeah.* Trusting Andy and taking him back the first time he cheated on her is the biggest. Marrying him is next. Having Frank catch her and Shane having sex last night sure wasn't ideal. And now tequila shots three through seven are quickly moving up the list.

But Shane? What a comforting, and surprisingly satisfying, find.

"None involving you."

"You're probably starving. Let's get dressed so you can eat." His warm kiss is almost as good as the view of his bare back and sculpted shoulders as he gets out of bed. Another serving of his body would be her breakfast if Frank wasn't standing in the living room right now.

The two wander from the bedroom, wearing plush, white hotel bathrobes and smirks for smiles. Their hot breakfast trays are on the table, Frank standing beside them.

"I know this is weird," Lauren says to Frank.

"Very," he grumbles.

"Hey, Frank, at least I got her to calm down last night," Shane says, pulling out Lauren's chair.

"You accomplished quite a bit in the four minutes I was gone," Frank says.

"Sacrificed myself as a human lime," Shane says with a winning smile.

"Ugh," Lauren says, "I don't even want to think about how much I drank." She lifts the round silver lid from a plate of scrambled eggs. *Total yum.* Before she dives in, she glances around her tray until she finds a small bottle of hot sauce. *Total awesome yum.*

"Hot sauce?" Shane asks, his eyes flashing humorous disbelief.

She lowers her eyes while shaking a few dashes onto her eggs. "Frank knows me almost as well as you do now." Shane smiles, reaches for the bottle and dashes hot sauce on his eggs too. Grinning, they each eat a forkful.

Frank shifts his weight. "I do need to talk with you."

"Go ahead," she says, biting a slice of dry toast. *Damn!* Her head pounds with every crunching bite. Maybe stick to eggs or something softer, like Oliver's remedy of muffins and milk.

"Privately?"

"Oh, secrets I can't hear," Shane says. "It's okay, I need to shower. You two talk." He stands but his eyes stay fixed on Lauren. Before leaving, he bends down to give her a kiss.

"Mmmm…you taste much better than this toast," she says, her eyes following him. She licks stray bread crumbs off her lips, wondering when Shane will invite her back under that robe. He does seem to enjoy taking control between the sheets. All night he decided how they'd do it and when they did it again. She never told him what she wanted. She never had to. Somehow he knew, and did it perfectly. She's never had a dominating lover like him before.

Frank glares at her as she watches Shane walk away.

She snaps out of her horny Shane-dream. "What's so secret that Shane can't hear?" she asks, sipping hot, delicious and life-saving coffee.

Frank sits down where Shane had been. His hands twist as he leans closer. "A lot has happened since we left New York."

"A lot has happened, period."

"Listen, something wasn't right with Andy when we saw him."

No shit. "A naked woman on my husband isn't normal?"

"We think something was put in his drink…"

"*No!*" she blurts. "I don't want to hear a crap load of Andy Hayden excuses. He did this before, *for days*, slept with another woman. He promised it would never happen again. I don't want to hear about a weak moment or a strong drink or any excuses!"

"This is real, Lauren."

"Stop. Frank. I'm moving on. I may have been drunk but I knew what I was doing and I'm not drunk now. Screw Andy!"

"He's on his way here."

"What? Here to Rome? Now?"

"He wants to talk with you."

"Too bad," she says, throwing her napkin on the table. "It's over, Frank. I'm not talking to him. I don't want to hear his crap."

"He and Ryan will be landing in about an hour. It would be good if you…"

"*No!*" she yells. "Hide me where he can't find me."

"Hide you?" Shane asks, walking out of the bathroom. He still hasn't started his shower.

"Andy's on his way here and I'm leaving," she says, getting up. "Let's find a place to go until he gives up and goes back home."

"You don't have a show until tomorrow night. We could go somewhere, maybe to the coast?"

"Perfect! Frank, find us somewhere you think is safe. A view of the water preferred and *don't* let Ryan know where we are."

Frank's eyes search for options. "I suppose if I try to keep you here, you will run."

"You bet I will. Just like at Christy's," she says, reminding him of the time when Andy suddenly appeared her at her best friend's house. Her raging run had everyone desperately trying to find her while her cut and bloody bare feet had her desperately wishing she had worn shoes. "And right now, Frank, I could run barefoot up the boot of Italy until I reach the Italian Alps to avoid Andy." Her stern glare dares him. "But this time, I've got shoes."

Frank swallows hard. "Be ready to leave in an hour."

* * *

The stiff breeze blows comfortably warm for a sunny August afternoon in Lido di Ostia. Lauren opens the balcony doors, stepping out for the fresh Tyrrhenian Sea air and a view of the black sand beach across the street. Her black lace tank top and shorts barely cover her skin underneath and it doesn't take long for Shane to grab her.

"God, this looks amazing on you," he says, slipping behind her, wearing only a pair of worn jeans.

"Thanks for buying it for me." She spins around, raising her arms to give him a view of her chest peeking through the lace. "I love all the clothes we picked out from the boutique downstairs."

"I'll buy you anything. Everything," he says, kissing her.

Sounds of the busy road below overtake the soft crashing of the waves on the beach. Their balcony gives them full access to the bright Italian sun while potted palm trees on the deck give them privacy.

They sit down together in a lounge chair, Lauren in between Shane's legs. Her eyes close with the warmth of the sun on her face. In a few hours, they'll need to decide what to do for dinner. She has a feeling that before dinner he'll decide to take her back to bed. She'll be ready when he does. She's ready now.

"I'm going to guess it's getting rough back in Rome," she says, gently stroking his leg. These faded jeans are such a departure from Shane's usual crisp, organized look. They're broken in and comfortable against her skin when she lies on him. Shane's softer side looks and feels good.

"You mean, Andy trying to figure out where you are?"

"I wonder if he knows about us yet."

"Don't care," Shane says. "I've been waiting a long time for my chance with you and now I have it."

She sits up, turning around to face him. How does he keep his hair so perfectly styled even after she's had her fingers all through it? "When was the first time you noticed me?"

"Noticed you? The first time I saw you! The first time you and Johnny walked into our office and handed over the movie soundtrack." He digs his wallet out of the back pocket of his jeans.

"What's that?"

He pulls out a small, folded picture. "I carry this everywhere."

She opens the folded photograph. "It's all of us! We took that photo after Plebeian's first concert. That was our first live TV concert to debut our first album!"

His smile fills with pride. "It was. Look, I was standing with my arm around you. I was so happy that night. The concert was so successful, but this, me holding you, was the best part."

Her hand rests on his bare shoulder, her other hand holding the picture. What irony! This picture was taken minutes after she had come face to face with Andy that night. Davis pulled her away from Andy so they could take this stupid photo of everyone. She hadn't seen Andy in years and all she wanted to do was get back to him and finish their conversation. Maybe her destiny was in this picture all this time. Maybe she should have spent more time that night with Shane instead of Andy.

"Every time there was a romantic opening in your life, I tried to get in."

"Romantic opening?"

"Let's start in Phoenix," he says. "Cory cheats on you but you leave in the morning before I have a chance to try to help."

"We did leave first thing the next morning. But you didn't know that I had already hooked up with Andy."

"I didn't. I knew you had a friend with you, but I thought I could be the one to help you the next day."

"That seems so long ago now."

"Then Andy went on a binge drinking romp with another woman in Ft. Lauderdale. Remember coming out to L.A. for that meeting to discuss the world tour?"

She nods. "I was in a pretty bad mood."

"And I was ready to get you out of that bad mood." He presses his forehead to hers. "We had dinner at Robert Burgess's home in Malibu that night. I was there before you. They had those fancy, gold pinecone place cards. I moved my name so I'd sit across from you."

"That's right! You were across from me! I was relieved you were there because I didn't have to worry about talking with you."

"Yeah, thanks," he says with a laugh. "Then Robert insisted Josh Spencer sit to your right. I was so mad he did that because sure enough, as soon as Josh sat down the two of you hit it off. Josh Spencer, the actor that he is, had all the right lines."

"You were jealous of Josh? But I thought the two of you have been friends for years."

"We have been. But he didn't know my feelings for you. No one did. And yeah, I was jealous. I might as well have been the salt and pepper shakers sitting across from you."

"Wow, Shane. I had no idea."

"It was hard for me on the world tour announcement trip—the cruise—when you surprised everyone with your wedding," he says, lowering his head. "I sat in the back of that church watching you walk down the aisle. I imagined it was me you were walking towards; me your smile was for. I dreamt it was us starting a new life. But I didn't quit; I knew someday I'd get you."

"Am I what you wanted for your birthday?"

"For my birthday...and Christmas, New Year's, Flag Day, St. Patrick's Day..."

"But, I don't get why you would wait for me. I mean, look at you! You are the man every woman wants: gorgeous, fit, irresistible, rich. Why haven't you dated anyone else?"

"Oh, now I've got to defend my romantic resume?" His playful fingers jab her stomach. "I've dated, plenty. Almost got married once. My career has always been my love, and what I've imagined with you."

She strokes his bare chest, bringing chill bumps to his skin. She smiles at the effect her touch has on him. "So, what exactly have you imagined with me?"

"Lauren, we are perfect for each other: your talent with my business skills," he says, his hands now gently holding her shoulders. "Now that Robert's gone there's no one to block my movie production company. With you by my side, we'll be one of the most powerful couples in Hollywood."

"Shane, I don't live in Hollywood."

"But you can! I'll buy us a house—on the ocean if you want."

"But I have kids!"

"They can come too! Together we can do anything we want!" He squeezes her shoulders.

"I'm not sure what I'm going to be doing after tomorrow night's concert, nevertheless my life plan."

"I know," he says, sliding his hand through her hair to hold her head. "I don't want to go too fast. I'm just so ready to move forward with you. I'm ready to keep you safe; to protect you like you're supposed to be protected."

"But Frank protects me just fine."

"Frank? Frank is a super nice guy, but come on. He left you alone when Andy ambushed you at your best friend's house and what happened? You got hurt. He wasn't even there the night you got shot! What kind of protection is that?"

"Shane!" she says, stiffening. "You don't know the details; what Frank and I discussed. We made decisions together on when he'd come with me and when he wouldn't. He didn't even know I had left the house the night I got shot. It wasn't his fault!"

"A stalker follows you for months and your security guy doesn't even notice him?"

"None of us noticed Clive Winters! Hell, I didn't notice him right in front of me during the Daytime interview in Boston and I knew him! Quit busting on Frank!" She scrambles off the chair, stomping to the railing and glaring at the beach across the street.

Seconds later, he's behind her. His fingers softly tickle her skin as he slips his hands around her waist. Her back arches, anticipating his moves. His touch, his kiss, his presence have become so addicting that even angry she can't resist.

"I'm sorry, Lauren. I have so much I want to do with you; so much I have been waiting to say. I guess I don't know how to say it right."

He nibbles softly at her neck. *Damn it, that feels so...Shane!* She rolls her head to give him more neck to nibble.

Lauren stands on a sunny deck in a beautiful Italian coastal town, her life now upside down. All the plans she had for her future have been scrapped; the man she married is probably wandering the streets of Rome in a panic to find her.

Instead, she's enjoying the erotic kisses of a man who has a new plan for her life. A man promising her the world: all new ideas and a powerful new direction. She's never released herself to a man who enjoys such control. It's not what she ever really wanted.

He is not Andy.

But his mouth on her neck is driving her crazy.

Her body buckles and twists with the apology of his lips.

She can't resist. "Please…"

His lips move to her ears. "Let's make up in bed."

Morning sounds of running water come from the bathroom.

"Hurry up or you'll miss breakfast," Lauren teases Shane.

"Get back in here so we can finish our shower!"

"Someone has to open the door for Frank or he'll just let himself in again," she says, pulling her white t-shirt over her wet hair. Steam is clouding Shane's view through the glass shower doors. *Perfect opportunity.* She tiptoes closer to the shower and steals his towel. That will get him back for taking her panties out of her suitcase and hiding them.

Three soft knocks means Frank has arrived.

Lauren scrunches her wet hair and opens the door.

"You are sweet to bring this up, but room service could have delivered this," she says. The simplicity of her shorts and fitted t-shirt convey her relaxed, rested mood. Not wearing any underwear is part of that relaxed feel but right now, it's not by choice.

Frank scans the room. He carries the tray to the table. "Shane's in the shower?"

"Yep, he knows you're coming. He'll be out in a second." She helps Frank unload their cereal, coffee and fruit.

"Lauren, are you okay?"

She breathes in dread. Not a lecture from Frank!

"I know this seems strange with me and Shane, but I'm happy right now. See? No fist," she says, holding up two open hands.

"I've been watching your hands, trust me. Listen, a lot is happening in Rome."

"And right now, I don't want to hear about it. That's why you have my phone. I don't want to take any calls. As long as the kids don't hear about this and try to reach me, there is no one I need to talk to. Lynette's a good publicist; she needs to keep a lid on this. All I want to know is when we leave here in three hours, Andy will be gone from Rome."

Frank doesn't say anything.

"Frank," she warns. "I will *not* go back to Rome if Andy is there. I'm serious. I don't want to see him. And if I don't get back to Rome this afternoon, that means no concert tonight."

"You could still do a show even if Andy was there."

"No," she says. "And since my record company president is in my bed I'm sure I would be excused."

"Can you just listen to what he has to say?"

"Look, last time Andy cheated on me I moped around for weeks. I was dazed and wimpy. It used to take me forever to come to terms with something, but not anymore. I've changed. Two bullets in the chest has made me hardcore, Frank. I'm not going to be a victim to anyone anymore. I was a victim to Andy once, but no more."

"It may not be what you think."

"Come on! Really? He left dinner with Ryan and within an hour had a girl in his bed. How many times has that happened while I've been gone? Is that why he hasn't been with me this entire tour? He's been 'taking care' of his financial clients? Is that what he wants to talk to me about? He wants to tell me I can trust him when he says that it won't happen again?"

"It's complicated."

She shakes her head. *No, it's not.* She just has new priorities now. Her old priority was proving that falling staircases and popping guitar frets were silly, freak coincidences on this bad luck world tour. Her new priority is figuring out how fast she can divorce her cheating husband.

"Shane and I are together. Andy and I are not. You make sure that Andy is gone by the time we get there."

Shane steps into the room, wearing a blue, waffle-weave hotel bathrobe. "Hey, Frank. Sorry I didn't make it out here faster. I couldn't find my towel." His eyes slowly shift towards Lauren. She smiles.

"I was just leaving. I'll be back in three hours to drive you to Rome." Frank turns to Lauren. "An Andy-free Rome."

"Perfect. Thank you," she says, seeing Frank to the door and closing it behind him.

She turns to Shane, who looks as delicious as the food he stands beside.

"I'm anxious to know what that was about," he says. "But first, I want to know who took my towel."

Oh crap. He reaches to grab her but she runs. He snatches her near the sofa and she willingly surrenders as her giggles confess. Together they fall on the cushions.

"You took my panties," she says, lying under her captor.

"What's wrong with that? You took my towel."

"And what's wrong with that?" Her fingers gently weave through his wet hair. "So…what are you going to take next?"

His devious eyes scan her. "I'm going to take you, right now."

Shane replaces the smile on Lauren's lips with one insanely slow kiss. His face glows with full blown enjoyment watching her body squirm underneath him. He bites his lip, then slowly grinds his hips against her.

Oh God. "Please…now," she whispers.

He shakes his head, flashing an evil grin.

No?? She's bursting.

"I will always give you what you want when you say please. But, right now, I'm going to take my time, taking you." His lips lower for another slow kiss while his hips slowly grind against her again. She writhes underneath him.

Cereal, coffee and fruit will apparently have to wait.

* * *

Plebeian's first Rome concert is in six hours.

Lauren's eyes dart around the hotel lobby as she, Shane and Frank return to their Rome hotel after their thirty hour coastal getaway.

"You promise he's gone," she asks Frank again, quickly walking through the lobby.

"Lauren—no ambushes," Frank says. "Andy left."

She scans her surroundings, not convinced that Frank would tell her the truth. She knows Frank would protect her life, but on this matter, she's not sure he's completely on her side. And she's not really sure why he's not.

She glances behind columns as they pass and she scans the faces of people sitting near the lobby bar. The registration desk looks clear; only one young family is checking in, their little boy entertaining himself by twirling his spinner suitcase. *Hurry*; get somewhere Andy can't jump out and surprise her.

Elevators in sight, she hears a loud *pop*. Her hands jolt to her chest as she gasps and spins around.

The little boy's spinning suitcase has crashed to the floor. He's unfazed, already picking it up. Lauren, on the other hand, is trying to remember how to breathe.

Frank is right by her side and Shane reaches for her.

"I just want to get out of this lobby," she mumbles.

They move faster to the elevators and arrive on the eighth floor. The elevator opens to the sounds of a power tool and Davis's voice.

"Put it on the bill. Thanks again," Davis says, shaking the hand of a man wearing a suit. Davis turns. He's not wearing his usual blue plaid shirt. He's wearing a gray long sleeve t-shirt. Does he even own anything but plaid shirts? *Wait.* That's Johnny's shirt!

Davis squares his jaw. "Well, look who's finally back," he says, anger seeping from his voice.

A hotel maintenance crew is finishing the installation of an eight-foot mirror outside the elevator.

"We're paying for hotel décor now?" Shane asks.

"Have to when one of our folks breaks it," Davis says. "Or to be more specific: the husband of one of ours."

"What happened?" Lauren asks.

"Does it matter?" Shane asks.

"I'd like to know."

"Got ugly with Andy," Davis says. "If you want to know more, ask me privately." He glares at Shane.

Oh my God, Andy was mad enough to break a mirror? Was he mad at himself because he caused this? Or mad when he found out about her and Shane? And why does Davis need to wear Johnny's clothes? But Shane's presence keeps her from asking more questions.

"I gotta get ready for the sound check," she says, walking away.

With each departing step she replays Davis's snarky voice. Maybe Andy isn't her only problem. Her relationship with Shane might not be going over well with the guys.

She turns the corner and her thought is confirmed.

Johnny is blocking the door of her suite.

"Glad to see you and your lover made it back in time for the show," he says, standing tall, arms crossed, face on fire.

Their eyes lock. Lauren's always been able to read Johnny's emotions through his eyes but right now anyone can see: he's glaring mad.

"I don't need crap from you right now," she says.

"If not now, then when?" Johnny asks.

"Back off, Johnny," Shane says, stepping closer.

"What the hell did you do, Shane? She was drunk and you took advantage of her?"

"I took *care* of her, Johnny."

"You're our record company president! You're supposed to take care of record sales, not sleep with the talent."

"Apparently it bothers you that I can do both."

Across from them, the door to Michael's suite opens. Michael steps into the hall.

Johnny points his finger at Shane. "She doesn't need *you* to complicate this."

"And I don't get a say in what I want?" Lauren yells.

Down the hall, Oliver steps out of his suite. "Oh my God, where's my popcorn?"

Johnny waves his hands in the air. "Of course you get a say but what you *don't* need is to *sleep* with the boss and be *kept* from the *truth*."

Across from Oliver, Doug's suite door opens. He steps into the hall, with Ashley and Amie peeking out behind him.

"What's the *truth* Johnny?" she yells. "Everyone knows now, right? Andy marched here to Rome and now everyone knows *his* side of the story. Did he tell you that he slept with another woman? Did he tell you that I caught him? Or did he tell you that *nothing is ever his fault*?"

Suite door 8168 opens and Bruce Sanders steps into the hall.

Davis intervenes. "We have less than five hours until our show; less than one hour until we leave. *None of this* gets decided *here* in a hotel hallway!"

"*Decided?*" she yells. "Why do *you* think *you* get to decide anything for *me*?"

Frank steps between Lauren and Johnny. He slips his key card into 8162 and opens her suite.

"This is gonna be the *angriest* show I've ever sung before!" she screams.

Johnny, Oliver, Michael, Davis and Doug stare at Shane. Ashley and Amie retreat from Doug's door but the curious eyes of Bruce Sanders still watch from the end of the hall.

Shane moves closer to Lauren and the open door. His face hovers inches away from Johnny's eyes of fire.

"There's nothing for you to worry about, Johnny," Shane says, his voice now calm. "I'll be taking care of Lauren now."

Shane lays an arm across Lauren's shoulders and guides her into the suite.

Frank follows, and closes the door.

[SEVEN]

"You've already made me miss a couple days of work," Shane says, trying to get out of bed the next morning. Lauren lies on top of him, valiantly fighting to keep him down.

"I am your work," she says, pushing his arms flat.

"That you are." His strong arms easily break her hold and he gently pushes her off of him to get out of bed. "If we're to conquer Hollywood, then you need to let me get back to my suite so I can do some work. This conference call I have this afternoon with Bruce and some of his investors may be the deal I've been waiting for."

Lauren rolls over on her stomach, defeated at her attempt to capture Shane and exhausted from last night's concert.

Critics have already declared last night's show the best of Plebeian's world tour. Lauren unleashed her anger on stage, screaming through parts of a few songs and stomping up and down the stage for most of the show. The tension between her and Johnny was on full display. Fans that used to start rumors about them getting back together seemed to love their obvious fighting. Twice she sang inches in front of Johnny's scowling face and one time she pushed him in the back during the hook of a song. She abandoned her stage fear and sunglasses and searched the crowd, looking for Andy, certain he was there no matter what Frank said. She put everything she had into last night's show, including some flirtatious bends and squats in Shane's direction, just to prove to the guys she was doing fine without Andy.

Now she only has twelve hours to recover before tonight's second, and final, show in Rome.

This really isn't the best day to go shopping.

"They've never asked and of all the days, this is the day they want me to go," she mumbles into her pillow.

Shane stands by the bed, threading his belt through the loops of his suit pants.

"It will be good for you to go shopping with Ashley and Amie," he says. "It will keep Johnny away from you."

"Johnny is so pissed I'm sleeping with you, trust me, I don't have to worry about him getting anywhere near me. We haven't talked since our little chat in the hall yesterday."

"Besides," he says, bending down to bury his face in her hair, "why don't you go buy yourself something special for me."

She turns over to face him. "For you?" She trails her fingers down his bare chest. "How about something for me to wear for you to enjoy?"

"That's exactly what I was hoping for."

"Then you can take it away from me so I'll have nothing to wear," she says, her finger still sliding down his smooth chest.

"That's my plan for every night."

Her face flushes. Anticipating what he'll do drives her crazy. For once she never has to think; she just does what he wants. But even though he controls what happens in bed, she knows how to lure him into it.

She wraps her hand around the back of his neck and pulls his head down. "Please?" she whispers.

He inhales deeply. "You drive me wild when you ask please," he whispers, half-leaning over her. "I will always give you what you want when you ask it."

"I wanted you to stay in bed in the first place," she whispers. "Come back to bed with me, please."

His belt unbuckles. His suit pants drop. He lifts up the top sheet, exposing her waiting, naked body. He slides down beside her. "Roll over," he says as she smiles.

"Are you excited for a day of shopping, Frank?" Lauren says, putting a quick spray of Shane's favorite perfume on her wrists.

"This is going to be a difficult day," he says.

She puts the perfume down and scowls. Good grief: shopping isn't difficult! It's not like she sends him into lingerie stores to buy her panties.

"Where are we meeting Amie and Ashley?" she asks, zipping her pink leather Fendi bag, a colorful compliment to her white jeans and black draped-front shirt.

"Downstairs," Frank says, opening the door.

A day of mindless shopping might be good to clear her mind. She's already thinking of what to surprise Shane with tonight. But moving to the forefront of her mind are two important calls she needs to make. She's got to figure out how, and how much, to tell the kids about Andy. She can call them now, or let them enjoy the last few days of their summer and tell them after the tour. Either way, she needs to call her attorney to discuss her next legal step.

The elevator opens and the two step inside. A man stands near the elevator buttons. The doors close, but Frank doesn't reach for the button.

"Frank, hit the lobby button," Lauren says.

Frank's face is straight; serious. His index finger rises to his mouth. "Shhhh."

What the heck?

Frank's free hand takes Lauren's purse off her shoulder. He looks again in her eyes.

"Shhh."

He hands the purse to the man.

The man turns, unzipping her purse and waving a flat electronic device the size of a desk stapler inside and around her bag.

Her heart pounds. *Frank?*

Frank nods with his finger still over his mouth.

Her eyes are as round as the elevator buttons, one of which lights up to announce their arrival on the fifth floor.

The man gives her purse back to Frank and leads them out of the elevator.

"What the hell…" she whispers.

"Lauren," Frank says, his hand on her elbow guiding her down the hallway as they follow the man. "I need you to trust me."

Her ears hurt from the nervous pounding in her chest. They stop outside room 564.

The man unlocks the door, holding it ajar so Frank can push it open.

Lauren steps backwards, scared that Andy is about to pop out from behind the door or something.

Frank reads her fear. "This isn't an ambush with Andy."

"Then what the hell do you call this?"

"I call this the most difficult day of your life." Frank pushes open the door.

She clenches her teeth; her body shivers with every curious step she takes into the room.

There, standing alone, next to two double beds in the dimly lit room, is Bruce Sanders.

[EIGHT]

Lauren squints. "Bruce?"

"Hello, Lauren," Bruce says, his signature, slicked-back hair neatly in place, his demeanor less abrasive than usual.

The door closes behind her. She turns to see Frank by her side. The strange man who led them here has disappeared.

Lauren scans the room for more surprises. "This is an odd way to start a day of shopping."

"You're not going shopping," Bruce says.

She looks to Frank.

"You'll want to sit down," Frank says, pulling out a chair from a writing desk.

She tentatively accepts the chair Frank is offering. Frank sits on the desk next to her while Bruce eases onto the edge of one of the beds.

"Okay," she says. "Who is going to tell me what's going on?"

Bruce leans forward, his hands folded and his eyes serious. "Lauren, a series of events has led to this meeting, and what I'm about to tell you needs to remain confidential."

She nods, swallowing a laugh. What's up with this drama? She's the lead singer in a rock band and her biggest problem is her busted marriage. Platinum Plate's investment value isn't going to tank because her personal life is a disaster. In fact, record sales usually soar when she has drama! Why is Bruce acting like there is some life-threatening issue?

Bruce continues. "I'm not an investor interested in the expansion of Platinum Plate records."

"Really? Then who are you?"

"I'm a Special Agent with the FBI."

She coils back. "FBI?"

Bruce nods.

Lauren turns to Frank. He used to work for the FBI, retiring after a twenty-year career hunting fugitives. Is that why Frank led her here to talk to Bruce?

She turns back to Bruce. "You've been with us most of the tour. Are we doing something wrong?"

"Oh, no. We wish all bands could be as legit as yours."

"Is it our string of bad luck?"

"That's been curious, but not why we started the investigation," Bruce says. "Lauren, we have been investigating the death of Robert Burgess."

"Robert?"

"We believe he was murdered."

"And you think we're involved?" she asks, quickly looking over to Frank. Why aren't Johnny and the guys here to listen to this?

"We know no one in your band did it," Bruce says. "But we think we know who did. We just need more evidence to prove it."

"So you followed our band half way around the world to solve a murder? I thought the FBI works on just about everything but murders?"

Bruce's jaw tightens. "We work on murder cases like this when it involves one of our own."

She sucks in a breath.

"As you and the others in Plebeian know, Robert was an established, successful businessman and a talented producer. He did very well as president of your Platinum Plate label. What you didn't know is that for years he served as one of our confidential human sources. Robert provided valuable information to us on various subjects over a long period of time. His death was suspicious to begin with, and because of the nature of what he was reporting to us at the time he died, we decided to investigate."

She gulps down what should have been a normal swallow. Maybe her life *does* involve life-threatening issues now. "So the fact that Robert had been working with you is something you want me to keep secret."

"Yes. Actually, I need you to keep everything we discuss secret."

"So why are you telling me this?"

"Because thanks to you, we may have gotten our luckiest break on this case a few days ago."

"Well, that's great I was able to help you with something I know nothing about," she says. "What was the break?"

"If I may be blunt, it was you finding your husband with another woman."

Her chin lowers. "What?"

Frank leans forward.

"I've been trying to tell you, when we found Andy, he wasn't right," Frank says. "Not right, meaning, drugged."

"No, no, no. It's way too late now to try to save my marriage."

"Lauren, please listen," Bruce says.

Frank continues. "I know that night was a blur and we left quickly, but Ryan contained the scene. He knew Andy's condition wasn't normal. He knew at dinner each of them only had one drink. Ryan had grabbed that woman's purse before she ran out the door. Inside the purse were some pills. Ryan guessed the woman slipped a crushed pill in Andy's drink before it was served, then got into his room."

Hearing this makes her shoulders heavier. Andy really was drugged?

"Ryan is smart," Frank continues. "Within minutes, he contacted Mary."

"Mary?" Lauren asks. "Who the hell is Mary?"

"Oliver's wife."

"Mary Brinks? Mary knows about pills?"

Frank nods. "She knows a lot about many things. She's an Intelligence Analyst with the FBI back in Tampa."

Lauren sits back. An FBI double whammy of surprises.

"All these years, I never knew where Mary worked. Is that why she's never around Oliver?"

Frank nods. "She travels a lot, and not just to avoid her husband. Oliver never talks about what she does, and only Johnny, Ryan and I knew she works for the FBI. Several years ago, Mary and I actually worked together on a public corruption case. We frequently talk about the past."

A clammy, sweaty feeling is forming on Lauren's body. Was that the message Oliver was trying to give her the night she got drunk? Listen to the facts? Did his wife tell him that Andy was drugged?

Frank continues. "So Ryan got Mary involved. Right away she made a call to the New York City field office. Those pills were on their way to the FBI lab for testing before you and I had even landed in Tampa."

Bruce picks back up. "Those pills they tested were barbiturates, we believe clearly intended to sedate Andy. Now, barbiturates are a common sedative, but we think there was a stronger connection. Mary had a theory, and when we found the key person in her theory, we found our break."

Lauren's face feels flushed, her heart pounding. "Who was the key person?"

"The woman you caught with Andy. And we did find her, dead."

"Oh my God! Someone killed her?"

"Yes," Bruce says. "She was poisoned with abrin, a highly noxious toxin similar to ricin."

"I've never heard of it," she says, shaking her head.

"It's not common," Bruce says. "And because it's uncommon it helped us make the connection. You see, Robert Burgess also died by inhaling abrin. It caused a seizure. He lost control and drove his car off that cliff. We found traces of abrin in his vehicle as well as in the woman's apartment. All it takes is a few sprinkles and in a few hours, the victim experiences flu-like symptoms, then hours later, sometimes a day or two later, death."

Lauren shifts in her chair, horribly uncomfortable with this topic. "So you think the person who drugged Robert is the same person who killed that woman?"

"Yes."

"And you think whoever killed them hired that woman to sleep with Andy?"

"Yes. Someone who benefitted from Robert's death. And someone who benefitted from drugging a married man and staging a woman on top of him."

Her eyes widen. "Oh, not…"

Bruce nods. "Shane Mitchell."

She twitches in disbelief, looking to Frank. His face is sad and serious, his eyes validating Bruce's words.

"This is about Shane?"

"Correct," Bruce says. "Shane has been the primary suspect in Robert's death since the beginning. Shane had everything to gain at Platinum Plate Records once Robert was out of the picture. He had tremendous access to Robert. They frequently dined together, including the night Robert died."

Lauren shakes her head. Words sort through her brain as she tries to take this in.

"But Shane is one of us! He's been around us since the beginning! Why would he do this?"

"He is a very ambitious man. He made no secret how eager he was to grow the label and expand the Platinum Plate brand, at a pace Robert Burgess did not want to do," Bruce says.

"Oh my God, Shane just told me how happy he was that Robert was out of his way so he could move forward with a movie production business with you!"

"That's exactly why I'm playing the part of investor," Bruce says. "I've been working to get a solid motive from Shane, and a confession."

"That leaves me."

Bruce nods. "He has been fixated on you since the beginning. I've obtained quite the insight on his motivation to get closer to you."

Her face feels slapped. "He told me he's wanted me since Johnny and I first walked into his office. He said he waited for romantic openings in my life. The Cory affair, when Andy left me…he laid out his game plan right in front of me and I didn't even pick up on it!"

Frank nods. "He probably got tired of waiting for his chance with you. This time, he controlled the situation."

"Shane knew I was going to New York to surprise Andy! He had hours to plan something while I was on the plane. I walked right into his trap!"

"And your reaction was probably what he wanted," Bruce says. "Shane wouldn't have wanted Andy dead, because you would have mourned Andy's loss for a long time. Drugging Andy and having you catch him in the act is a much faster way for Shane to get you."

"And getting rid of the woman he hired is just part of the clean up," Frank adds.

Lauren rubs her face. Shane? Murder? Drugging? Accidents? This is unbelievable. This is so much information, so much betrayal, so much…

"OH MY GOD, ANDY!" she screams, jumping up, slapping her hands to her face. "Andy! I cheated on Andy to get back at him and *he didn't do anything wrong!* He was trying to find me, to tell me he didn't do anything wrong! *I ran from him!"*

Frank grabs her. She's an instant, hysterical mess, emotions unraveling with the speed of her thoughts.

"Lauren!" Frank yells, squeezing her shoulders.

She shakes uncontrollably. Layers of her stupidity peel back with every revelation. She's made a bigger mess of her marriage than Andy ever has!

"Andy didn't do anything wrong! Why didn't you let Andy get to

me? If you knew Shane was behind all this, why didn't you tell me?"

"I couldn't allow Andy to get to you," Bruce says.

"*Allow?*" she screams, twisting out of Frank's hold.

"I had to get Andy out of here," Bruce says.

Her hands flail in the air; she stomps in an aggravated pacing.

"Andy was here, trying to tell me he was drugged, and you *took him*?" she yells.

"His search for you was calling a lot of attention to the situation," Bruce says calmly. "We had just discovered the murdered woman and needed more time to sort through our facts."

"*You* needed *time*? What did you do with Andy?"

Bruce's face is solid. Lauren's melts.

"*Where* is Andy?" she demands.

"He was arrested," Bruce says.

"*What?* You had Andy *arrested*?"

"I had to. Andy hit this town on a tear to find you. He fought with Davis in the hall. In fact, Davis needed stitches in his arm after Andy threw him into the mirror by the elevators. Johnny, Oliver and Doug—everyone was trying to calm Andy down when he found out about you and Shane. All Andy knew when he arrived in Italy was that he had been drugged from the barbiturates found in that woman's purse. On his own he guessed that Shane was behind it. Too many people were starting to get too mad at Shane. Though they have no proof, everyone now thinks the events were too coincidental and that Shane drugged Andy to get closer to you."

Lauren lowers her head. That's why Johnny and Davis were so mad! They spent the day dealing with an enraged Andy while she lounged on the Italian coast, blissfully enjoying a day of sun and sex with Shane.

"But why? Why arrest Andy?"

"It was my only way to get him removed without anyone knowing who I am. And more importantly, to keep him from coming back," Bruce says.

"*Your* only way? Who put *you* in charge of our lives??"

The small hairs on the back of Lauren's neck bristle in anger; her constant pacing has worn a path in the carpet.

"We needed more time," Bruce says.

"Time? Oh my God!" She turns to Frank. "You've got to take me to Andy right now. Is he in jail?"

Frank shakes his head. "No, he's not in jail. He's safe."

"Lauren," Bruce says, his hands pressing the air, trying to calm her down. "Our legal attaché worked with our foreign partners here. They pressed charges, only to drop those charges once he agreed to leave the country."

"Where is Andy now?"

"Safe," Frank says. "He's at your Kiawah Island home. We convinced him to stay away from Tampa for a few days. Ryan has him safe at Kiawah."

"The kids! The kids still don't know any of this, right?"

"They don't know anything. Cory has the boys, Janie has Brittney. The summer calendar for the kids hasn't changed," Frank says.

She clenches her jaw, grinding her teeth in disgust. "You did this so Andy can't legally come back to Italy, didn't you?"

Bruce nods. "Correct."

"I don't understand! Why are you trying to keep Andy from me?"

"Because this is not over, yet."

[NINE]

Lauren stiffens with Bruce's words. "What do you mean, not over yet?"

"Just because you know we're investigating Shane Mitchell for Robert Burgess's murder doesn't mean we've closed the case," Bruce says. "I don't have a confession or even a rock-solid motive."

"This is a nightmare!" she says. "I've got to talk to Andy."

"No, you can't," Bruce says.

"Oh, yes I can." She reaches for her purse but Frank grabs her arm.

"Lauren, you have got to hear Bruce out. There is more."

Her shoulders melt. "No, no…I can't handle any more."

Just thinking about Andy makes her lightheaded, as though every drop of blood in her body has drained to her feet. He's forced to sit at the beach house, knowing he was drugged and caught in bed with another woman, which pushed her to sleep with another man! Her emotions start to gear up again, her heart beating faster. And then it hits her why they want to keep her and Andy apart.

"Oh no. You are not going to ask me to…you are not going to ask me to try to get information from Shane…"

Bruce's eyes tell her the answer. Yes.

"Oh no…no," she says, rapidly shaking her head.

"You are the closest person we've ever had to Shane. Even after months of me pretending to be Bruce Sanders I've never gotten as close as you are now. We need you to try, Lauren, just try to get some information so we can solve these murders."

"Oh no…I don't ever want to *see* Shane Mitchell again. I can't pretend I still want to sleep with…oh my God, *no!*"

"You don't have to sleep with him," Bruce says.

"I'm supposed to do…what? Just hang out with him? Shane and I were doing it like three to four times a night!"

Frank winces.

"No!" she pleads. "I can't do this!"

"We can help you," Bruce says. "I will teach you what to ask and show you how to act. You will have a listening device to record everything he says."

Training? They provide on-the-go, day courses in spy training? A *"How to ask your lover if he's a murderer before reaching climax"* class?

What is she supposed to do?

She steps backwards and collapses in the safety of the chair. Shock stings her crumpled body.

"Lauren," Frank says, sitting back on the desk. "Put Andy aside for a minute. Even if you broke it off with Shane today, Shane doesn't go away. He's still the president of your record company. He'll still be here on tour. The only way to remove him is to help Bruce get the evidence he needs."

Frank. He *does* know her so well. He knows right and wrong so well, too. And now, he's right. She's got to think of team Plebeian. Her eyes close, her head falls into her hands. Her mind fills with images of her friends, some she's known for years.

Davis: her college friend and favorite coworker at the Riverside Resort hotel. In the beginning she used to answer the switchboard and he filed bills. They celebrated his first paycheck by splurging on a steak dinner and a shopping trip, where he proudly bought an $89 pair of blue, leather-laced boat shoes. Now Davis manages Plebeian, with stitches in his arm from a fight with her husband. He fought to calm Andy down, not realizing that by doing so he was helping the plan to capture a killer.

Oliver: her antagonist since the band's beginning; Johnny's friend that she often cannot stand. He tried to warn her to listen to the truth at a time she didn't want to hear it. His wife Mary worked in the middle of the night to process information that exonerated Andy and identified a killer.

Michael: her friend from church. His fingers played musical magic while she sang the solos. He believed even before the tour started that their band was in the presence of evil. He tried to get her to listen, to connect these events to the hands of a killer.

Doug: her son's percussion teacher and their silent slayer on the drums. He looks to her as an example as he struggles with the news that soon he'll be a father. What example does she set for him if she doesn't do her part to capture a killer?

Lynette: her other coworker at the Riverside. Lynette shared a cubicle with her when she was promoted to the marketing department. They jokingly wrote scandalous press releases as office pranks, giving managers a scare that this was the news they were sharing to the media. Now, Lynette is the publicist protecting her, managing the scandals of her life. Thanks to Lynette, no one knows she has been sleeping with a killer.

Frank: her protector. He would do anything for her. Despite what Shane thinks, Frank has always served her well. Frank kept her safe, even when she was in bed with a killer.

Max: the carefree, talented twenty-four-year-old who lost his father. Max is now home recovering from a broken leg but it was Max who helped her heal after she was shot. He used his experience from college theatre and voice classes to teach her how to fill her scarred lung with breath for song. She trusted him at a time when she was too frightened to trust doctors or anyone else she didn't know. He rewarded Lauren's upbeat attitude during that difficult time by giving her a nickname: Chipper. His loyalty to Lauren was one of the reasons Johnny asked him to join Plebeian on guitar. Could she bring Max closure if she helped catch his father's killer?

And Johnny: her college lover and the man who chose her as the lead singer. This band is Johnny's dream. If she doesn't get this information, Plebeian will remain in danger. Their contract keeps Shane involved. She's got to do her part to cut Plebeian's ties with this killer.

Lauren opens her eyes, looking down to her lap. Her breathtaking, seventy-hour romance with Shane must end. She gave her body to him in an act of defiance. She was surprised by Shane's deep affection for her, and the searing level of pleasure he offered. Her heart was just opening with love. He promised to give her the world, but it was his world, his dream. Of course it was. All of this was his plan. He manipulated events to win her. She fell into a trap where his pleasure dominated her. What would have happened if she disagreed with his plan? What if she ever left him? Would she end up with a crushed pill swimming in her drink? Or a dash of poison powder on her microphone?

Her eyes find Bruce's.

"I'll do it," she says. "But I have one request."

"Name it."

"I have to talk to Andy first."

Bruce shakes his head. "Andy cannot know about this."

"But I need to talk to him."

"Andy cannot know we are investigating Shane for murder."

"One call?" Frank asks. "Only for her to tell him she knows New York City was not his fault and that she's not with Shane anymore."

"Can't happen," Bruce says. "She cannot bring Andy into this circle."

"Fine, Bruce. Then I walk out of this room and call him," she says, standing up.

Bruce squares his jaw.

She reaches for her purse. "I get that you're undercover. I get that no one can know you are investigating a murder. And I promise I'll never tell anyone that. But until I can talk to Andy and make things right, you don't 'get' me."

His cheeks pulse in an irritated throb.

"One call," he says, "only to discuss those two things."
Her head rises, surprised.
Bruce walks towards the door, turning to face her before he leaves.
"Use Frank's phone. You have five minutes."

[TEN]

Lauren stands alone with Frank in the deafening silence of room 564.

This feeling of embarrassment and hurt standing in front of Frank isn't new. Neither is this dreaded feeling of what she must do next. A long time ago at Christy and Cal's, after she ran away from Andy, the most difficult apology she had to make was to Frank. He didn't deserve her stupidity when she insisted she drive there alone. He didn't deserve to race across the state of Florida in a rush to find her. She even turned off her phone tracker to hide from him. He didn't deserve to not have the chance to do his job.

And now, here she stands, alone with Frank, needing to apologize again.

"Frank," she whispers, swallowing hard. "I'm so sorry I didn't listen to you. You were trying to tell me but I didn't want to hear it. I can't believe I fell for Shane's trap."

"You were emotionally swept away; I know the signs. I have seen this with others during my career."

"Shane was even trying to get me to think you were a bad security person because I was shot under your watch."

"I knew I'd be his target at some point," he says, glancing down to his phone as he finishes a text. "That's what guys like Shane do. They slowly take people you trust out of your life, so all you have left is them. That's why I went along with you to Lido di Ostia, even though

I wanted to keep you here in Rome. I had to pretend I was on board. That's also why I kept delivering your room service meals. It was my only way to check on you to be sure you were okay."

"Man, I need to give you a raise," she says, sniffing back tears. "Ryan too."

"We wouldn't still be here unless we believed in you and Andy," he says. "Ready?"

She rubs her face. *No…she isn't ready; now or in a hundred years from now.* How exactly is she supposed to start this call? Hi honey, what's new? Weather is great in Italy, too bad you can never come back? Good news: I've learned some tricks in bed that we should try? Her head drops.

"I don't even know where to start."

"Do you want a video call?"

"*No!* I can't look at Andy right now. I'm…I'm so embarrassed."

"Lauren, I'm sure he is too. Remember, we all watched him fall out of bed naked."

She cracks a halfhearted smile. "We have no secrets left in this family."

Frank raises his phone. "Yes, you do. Don't forget, you cannot tell Andy about Bruce or the murder investigation."

"But Bruce isn't here now. Why can't I tell Andy everything?"

"The more people that are brought into an undercover operation, the more you risk ruining the operation. Andy is important to you, but he's not an asset to the murder investigation. He cannot know."

"How long have you known all this?"

Frank looks down. "It's unfolded in pieces for me. I knew Andy was drugged and Mary was involved by the time we arrived in Rome, and I tried to tell you then. But I didn't know about Bruce until after your fight with Johnny in the hallway yesterday. Bruce realized the situation is escalating and it was only a matter of time until Andy got to you. I insisted that you be told; I don't want you alone with a suspected killer, unless you are a willing participant in this operation.

Bruce needs your help and knows he has to move quickly now."

She nods, wringing her hands.

"I just texted Ryan and he's expecting this call. Ryan will give his phone to Andy and I'll give you mine. I'll be right outside the door. Remember Lauren, you have a lot to learn this afternoon, plus you have a concert tonight. We don't have a lot of time."

Her heart races with each digit Frank presses. The man she hated an hour ago is the man she'll be begging forgiveness from in moments. How can she ever begin this call?

"Hey, Ryan," Frank says, watching Lauren. "She's ready."

Her breathing has stopped waiting for Frank to speak, knowing the next time he does Andy will be on the phone. She will be one step closer to the biggest apology of her life.

"Hi, Andy. I've got Lauren here, hold on."

Frank extends his phone. Her eyes cross, looking at his phone like she's never seen one before. Slowly, she takes it. Frank smiles, and leaves the room.

She's all alone, holding a phone connecting her to the love of her life. To the innocent man she just cheated on, the man she'd wished was lying in the same bed when she plunged a knife through a defenseless pillow. Now, she has a lot of explaining to do.

She swallows hard and slowly slides down to the floor between the two double beds. She belongs on the floor; she feels like scummy dirt.

"Lauren?" she hears Andy's voice call her, even though the phone isn't near her ear.

She swallows again, and then raises the phone.

"Andy?" she whimpers.

He breathes. "Oh, Lauren."

"Andy, I don't know where to start..." she whispers when tears hijack the call. She sobs like a child, deep from her stomach, from her heart. Her words come out in pieces as she cries. "I'm. So. Sorry."

Tears roll down her cheeks, her body as flimsy as a ragdoll on the hotel room floor.

"Lauren, this isn't your fault. I was drugged. You've got to believe me; I didn't know what was going on. What you did after you saw me, it isn't your fault."

"I cheated on you! I ruined our marriage! I did everything wrong!"

"No baby, you fell into a trap. You were tricked; we've both been tricked!"

"You didn't do anything wrong and I did. I ruined our marriage!"

"No, you didn't! I'm still here! Lauren, I'm still here!" he insists.

Her face and nose drip with tears as she listens to the man she loves now desperately trying to calm her.

"I'm still here, Lauren. I'll never leave you. I'm still here."

Her breathing stills but her heart races. She awkwardly sniffles in a wad of snot.

"I'm ending it. I just wanted you to know I'm ending everything with Shane."

"I think Shane arranged to have me drugged. His timing was too perfect. I think he did this to win you."

"I'm going to try to get him to admit some things."

"No!" Andy says. "Don't even be alone with Shane! Keep Frank with you at all times. If Shane had someone drug me he could easily do something to you. Don't try to prove anything. Just stay away from him until I come back to Europe."

"But Frank said you were arrested and can't come back."

"Just Italy, baby. I'm not allowed back in Italy. But the tour goes to Austria in three days and there's nothing that can stop me from being there."

"In…Austria?" Her words slur as a new panic begins to form.

"Yes. I will be there and I will deal with Shane then."

Her heart thumps. *Holy shit, this isn't good.* Her timetable to get Shane's confession just moved up. She can only get Shane's confession if she pretends she's still with him, and she can't pretend to be Shane's lover if Andy's back! Her head pounds in conflict: she desperately wants to see Andy but she knows without Shane's confession, none of their problems get solved. In fact, if Andy comes face-to-face with Shane, their problems might only get bigger! If Andy hurts Shane he might get arrested for real or even worse, Shane might do something horrible to Andy. This is a mess within a mess and it's all her fault.

"Andy, I am so sorry for what I've done." Even if she says this a thousand times she still won't feel she's said it enough.

"Lauren, we will work through this. You can tell me everything; every little detail so there will be no secrets between us. I told you everything when I had secrets. I sat on the floor and repeated the disgusting details of every horrible thing I had done. You will tell me and I will move past it. We will move past this together."

Her mouth trembles. "I love you, Andy," she whispers.

"Lauren, I love you."

She sniffles again, turning to wipe her face on the side of the comforter.

Soft knocks on the hotel room door mean that her time with Andy is over.

"I have to go. Andy, things here are complicated, and I'm not sure when I will call you next."

"Lauren…please…stay away from Shane."

She can't! And now she has another new secret: she can't tell Frank and Bruce that Andy will be coming back in three days, or Bruce might find some bogus reason to have Andy arrested in Austria too.

Frank and Bruce walk back in the room.

No! She doesn't want to hang up! She wants to jump through the phone into Andy's arms but once again there's some imaginary line keeping them apart. An imaginary line once kept them apart while Lauren struggled in her marriage with Cory and Andy tried to keep his love for Lauren a secret. Andy crossed that line with kisses in a hot tub in Phoenix on the day they first made love. An imaginary line came between them again when Andy left her, but Lauren crossed it when she forgave him during an intimate retreat in Mexico. If a situation draws a line to keep them apart, one of them always ends up crossing it. But right now, the line between them seems harder than ever to cross.

"Andy," she holds the phone closer, whispering so Frank and Bruce can't hear, "I know there is this line between us, and I respect that, but I want you to know…"

"Lauren," Andy interrupts their familiar exchange, "I'm going to cross that damn line like a wild man and cover you with kisses when I see you next."

His words are so comforting that she manages a smile. "I love you, Andy. Even when I was mad at you and hated you, I loved you."

"Lauren, remember, I love you more than I can ever make you know."

The call ends.

Watching the dimming phone screen pulls the air out of her lungs. She raises her knees and buries her head in her crossed arms, her ears ringing with the sound of Andy's voice. Her heart feels shattered. And somehow she's got to be clever enough to get Shane to confess to a horrible crime. Fast. But right now, she can't even lift her body off the floor.

Frank reaches for his phone. "Ready?"

She inhales a cleansing breath and hands him the phone.

"I'm not sure I can do this," she says, looking up.

Frank kneels down. "Ultimately, it's your call. And I work for you, not the FBI. It's my job to keep you out of danger, and trying to get Shane to confess could put you in harm's way. I'd rather keep you safe, but I also know you. A day will come that you'll look back at this moment, and you'll want to say you did this."

She nods. There is no choice. She's got to get rid of Shane, before Andy does.

"Let me get off my ass and get to work."

Frank offers her a steady hand. She grabs it and they both stand up.

"I don't have a lot of time to prepare you," Bruce says. "I've got to get back to my suite for this staged conference call with Shane this afternoon. After we're finished, Shane will want to get back to you."

She nods.

"And I need to leave right now," Frank says. "I've got to find Ashley and Amie."

"Oh no! That's right! I was supposed to be shopping with them today."

"I texted them earlier to say you couldn't come. But I need to talk with them now and explain how you needed to be alone today. I will ask them to say you were with them all day if Shane asks," Frank says. "Trust me, no one wants anything to do with Shane right now, so I am sure Amie and Ashley would help with an alibi."

Lauren nods. Amie and Ashley would do that. Even though she's not close to them, she knows they would help a woman having a man crisis.

Her eyes hurt watching Frank walk towards the door, wishing she could go with him instead of staying here. "Frank?"

Hand on the doorknob, he turns.

"You were right," she says. "This is the most difficult day of my life."

He nods.

The door closes behind Frank and the room temperature drops. Her body aches with sudden chills with what she just realized. Not only is she without her protector, now she's all alone in a hotel room with Bruce Sanders. Or whatever his real name is.

"Okay, Lauren," Bruce says. "We've got to get to work."

Now she must listen and learn from a man she cannot stand. Only a few days ago she wanted to throw up watching this man swagger over to her table. Now, she must trust him. The tables have definitely turned.

She needs Bruce now. He will show her everything she needs to capture a killer.

And ultimately, he will get her back to Andy.

[ELEVEN]

Lauren's breathing stills, the quiet of her suite broken only by the muffled sounds of a vacuum servicing Michael's suite across the hall.

She sits on the sofa like a frozen block of ice, her terrified mind racing as she stares at the coffee table in front of her. On the table is her pink leather Fendi bag.

That bag carries the solution to her problems.

Inside it is a new lipstick. It's not her shade, because it's not really lipstick. It's a recording device. As long as she keeps it near, everything Shane says will be recorded. And the faster she can get Shane to tell her what Bruce needs, the faster this will be over.

She'd prefer if every lampshade, every picture on the wall, every corner of this suite were embedded with a listening device. But that gets tricky for the FBI since they're in a foreign country. A listening device placed inside moveable personal effects, however, is a different story.

With three hours until their caravan leaves for tonight's concert, she is already wearing her red skinny jeans and black leather sleeveless shirt. Dressing early in her stage clothes means she doesn't have to change in front of Shane.

It took ten minutes for her to wash her wrists, scrubbing off the perfumed scent that drives Shane crazy. The word "please" has been removed from her mental vocabulary.

Two props have been left in plain view on the bathroom counter: a box of tampons and a bottle of pain pills. Tonight she plans an academy-worthy performance to fake the mother-of-all-menstrual periods to avoid intimacy with Shane.

Soon, he'll be finished with his meeting with Bruce. Time is running out to prepare. Time is running out to process everything she learned during this horrible day. The weight of it all makes it hard to breathe.

It's times like this when she needs Andy's comforting arms. But instead, she'll be terrified in the arms of Shane. She has to wrap herself in his arms to get back into the arms of the man she really loves.

Three soft courtesy knocks interrupt her thoughts. *No! Already? Is it Shane?*

Frank opens the door and steps inside. "Johnny's here."

She jumps up, shaking her head. "Do I have time? Should I talk to him?"

"You have time. But remember Lauren, you can't tell him about Bruce," he whispers. She nods.

Frank turns to let Johnny in and a wave of panic overtakes her. Her purse! She didn't agree to have *all* of her conversations recorded! She snatches the bag, rushes into the bathroom, wraps the purse in a towel and stuffs it inside the bathroom cabinet. For good measure, she closes the bathroom door, and then the bedroom one. Out of breath, she comes face to face with Johnny walking in.

His hands are tucked into the pockets of his jeans, his black, vintage-wash t-shirt looks normal but his face looks taut with anger. "I want to talk about what happened yesterday."

The sight of Johnny unglues her. *Damn this acting stuff.* She runs to him. His face softens and he opens his arms. She falls into them.

"I'm so sorry about yesterday," she says, buried against his chest. "I'm so sorry for all the trouble I've caused."

Johnny squeezes her. "I know Frank has been trying to tell you, but you've got to listen. Andy was drugged. Someone put something in his drink and we all are starting to think Shane was involved."

She pulls away from him, wiping her eyes and nodding. "I know. I think Shane might have been involved too."

"This relationship with Shane isn't good for you."

"I know," she says. "I'm working on what to do next. You have to trust me."

"Working on what to do next? You break it off with Shane. That's what you do next," he says. "No good can come from sleeping with the boss. Like, ever."

"It's not that easy."

"Why? What else is going on?"

She steps away, moving to sit on the sofa. He follows, sitting beside her.

"Lauren, all of us think Shane staged some woman in Andy's bed so you would see it. In fact, we think all the bad luck on this tour has Shane's name written all over it."

She stiffens. *Wait.* Could Shane be behind *all* of their bad luck? How the heck did they come up with that?

Johnny whispers, "We think Shane's got people that have done all kinds of things, like rigging the stairs for Max to fall."

Oh no. Now that's getting ridiculous. They don't know the facts, and the facts are much worse than falling staircases. Shane wants to make money; he's way too ambitious to mess up a money-making tour. She can't listen to this. If Johnny even breathes the words "Robert Burgess" she'll crack.

"Look," she says, "I'm awake now, okay? I get it. I'm working on it. It's complicated and I just need you to understand."

He leans towards her, looking into her eyes. Their glances lock in that way that they do. So many messages their eyes have always been able to send.

His are saying he will help her.

Hers try to say *Shane is a murderer who killed two people with a powder she already forgot the name of. Drama from falling staircases is not the largest issue. If she doesn't get Shane to confess before Andy arrives in Vienna, Andy might also end up committing a murder.* But it's a little much for her to communicate in one look.

Three soft knocks interrupt them. Frank comes in.

"Sorry to interrupt," Frank says. "Lauren, I just saw Shane in the hall heading to his suite. His meeting with Bruce is over. I thought you might like to know he'll be here soon."

Shit! She jumps to her feet. "You need to leave," she snaps to Johnny.

"Um…okay…" he says, slowly getting up. "See you in a little bit for the ride to the arena."

She pulls his arm to lead him to the door, not even looking at him to say goodbye before turning away. There's no time for social graces. She's got to get her purse!

Flustered, she dashes to the bedroom, flinging open the door. She plows through the bathroom door, opens the cabinet, grabs the purse and throws the towel to the floor before she runs back to the living room.

She plops the purse on the coffee table, nervously adjusting the pink bag as if it were an artful centerpiece, then nudging it to be sure it's as close to the couch as possible. *Stay on the couch. Do not let Shane lure you to the bedroom. And for God's sake: don't say please!*

Frank's typical three knocks sound from the door.

It's show time.

If her heart would stop pounding, she might be able to catch her breath. She closes her eyes, wishing herself good luck, the same good luck move she did at the Academy Awards, moments before Plebeian went live and introduced themselves to the world. It worked that night. Please, good luck, be here tonight.

Frank opens the door. "Lauren, Shane is here."

"When are you going to reward me with my own room key?" Shane asks, stepping inside and greeting her with a kiss that warms her lips but chills her soul.

"Maybe when you finally earn it," she jokes. "Thanks, Frank," she says with desperate eyes before Frank closes the door. She pulls in a big breath, then turns to Shane. "So, how'd your big meeting go?"

"Amazingly well. Bruce is close to coughing up the cash for me," he says, pulling her closer for another kiss.

Actually, Bruce is close to coughing up a pair of handcuffs for him, if she's lucky right now.

Shane pulls back, looking her over. "Am I late or are you ready early?"

"I'm ready early," she says, holding his hand and leading him to the sofa. "I feel like crap and I was hoping if I was in my stage clothes it would make me feel like the show must go on. If you're not too busy, can you lie down with me?"

"You never have to ask me twice to get horizontal with you," he says, taking off his suit jacket. He stretches out beside her and pulls her into his arms. "Was it something you ate?"

She lays her head on his crisp, white dress shirt and curls to his chest, an intimate position Bruce suggested so she doesn't have to look into Shane's eyes.

"I don't think so," she says. "This is more like I'm about to bust open in the biggest period of my life, nauseous feeling."

"Ohhhh…that's something I can't help you with."

She squeezes him. Only hours ago a cuddle like this would have turned into sex. Now, she has no appetite for foreplay with a murderer. Time is ticking and her lipstick is listening.

"You really would help me with anything, wouldn't you?"

"Now that you're mine, I'd do anything for you."

"What would you do if I didn't feel safe?"

"Lauren, I'd do anything necessary to protect you. What is it?"

She nuzzles closer to his chest again. *Think! Fast!*

"Just something the girls told me today. Messages from Andy."

Shane sits up, breaking their cuddle. "Andy's trying to send you messages?"

She pats his chest to calm him and pushes him flat to lie on him again.

"It's okay. I'm not listening to what he has to say. I just want him to go away."

"Don't listen, Lauren. Don't trust whatever Andy is trying to say."

"Have you ever had a problem, a *big* problem, you wished would go away?"

Her heart races. *Bite the bait, Shane!*

"There's no problem I can't get rid of," he says.

Perfect! Her heart thumps. Now, get him to say how he's gotten rid of problems before!

"What would you…" she says but he interrupts.

"I don't want to talk about problems, I want you to rest."

Crap! No! Get back on the subject!

"But, how do you…"

"Shhh," he says in a hissing voice. "You don't have much time before the show. Let's rest. You'll need your energy for the concert. And extra energy for what I plan to do to you later tonight."

He kisses her hair. Her scalp feels seared.

Just this morning if Shane had mentioned plans to do something to her, she'd be fully aroused in anticipation. Now his dominance is frightening. It's also making her sick. If she could hurl on cue, she'd vomit *right now.*

Lauren lies still, listening to the beating of Shane's heart. She's got to get back on topic. She has to get him to admit he's capable of murder and that he's done it before. But right now, she's got nothing.

Round one has failed.

* * *

Applause from grateful fans rocks the arena as Plebeian finishes their last encore and waves goodbye to Rome. Johnny, Lauren, Michael, Doug and Oliver rush off stage for their traditional post-concert huddle.

"You seemed a little off tonight," Oliver says, smacking Lauren in the shoulder as they walk off stage.

"Give her a break," Michael says, walking beside them. "If you were sleeping with the boss who probably drugged your husband, you might be off too."

"Both of you shut up," Johnny says, seeing Davis ahead.

They are greeted by Davis's terror-stricken face.

"Straight to the van," he barks, pointing to a passenger van on the loading dock.

"We always huddle first," Michael says.

"Not tonight." Davis thrusts his pointed finger towards the van.

Thundering applause from the crowd begging for another encore makes it difficult to hear backstage.

"Davis?" Johnny asks.

"The van. Now."

Lauren quickly glances around the backstage area. *What's going on? Where's Frank?* She follows the others and bends to step into the van. Davis pushes her inside and she smacks her head on the roof of the van.

"Frank!" she says, seeing him behind the wheel. She rubs her head. "Where's the Italian driver?"

Davis stuffs Johnny in beside Lauren, and then jumps in the front passenger seat.

"Like a bat out of hell, Frank, *roll*!" Davis yells.

Frank crushes the gas and the van peels out of the loading dock.

Johnny, Lauren and Michael smash together in the middle seat while Oliver and Doug roll around the third row. What happened to not rolling without seatbelts since Dallas?

Lauren glances out the window and sees Shane, abandoned on the back dock.

Frank weaves in and out of traffic.

"Are we in that big of a hurry to get to Milan?" Johnny asks.

"We aren't going to Milan," Davis says.

"One of you needs to talk. Now," Johnny says.

"I'm shutting down this voodoo tour," Davis says.

"*What?*" Johnny yells. "You can't do that!"

"I'm the manager of this band and yes I can!" Davis yells back.

"What's going on? Why now?" Michael asks.

Davis is silent.

"Where are we going?" Johnny asks.

"The airport. The charter flight is ready," Davis says.

"Wait! Where are Amie and Ashley?" Johnny yells.

"I put them on a charter an hour ago with all of your stuff. Your hotel rooms have been cleaned out. We're heading home."

"*Davis!* Have you gone mad?" Johnny yells. "We have shows to do in *eight more cities!*"

Lauren hasn't been paying much attention to their yelling. Something else has her attention. While Frank has been driving, he keeps glancing in the rearview mirror at her. In the mere seconds of each glance, he blinks hard. That's the signal: something is terribly wrong but she has to remain calm.

While Johnny yells about disappointed fans, her heart pounds hard. Her sweaty concert clothes feel icy against her skin.

"There's *no way* we could have finished the next eight shows," Davis yells. "I'm shutting the tour down. The evil is real and it stops *tonight!*"

Frank glances back to Lauren and blinks slow. She stares at him. *Remain calm.*

"*Why* the hell can't we finish the last shows?" Johnny asks.

"Because we wouldn't have a lead singer!" Davis blurts.

The van quiets.

Frank's blinking has prepared her. She takes a steady breath in.

"Davis," she softly says. "What happened?"

Davis faces forward, the van speeding towards the airport. He pounds the dashboard.

"They got to Andy."

Her hands jolt to her face. Johnny bends towards Davis to better hear. Michael's breathing has stilled. It doesn't even seem like Oliver and Doug are in the van.

She slowly licks her suddenly dry lips. *Stay calm.* "What do you mean…got to Andy?"

Davis faces her.

"Some goons busted into your Kiawah home. Andy and Ryan were beaten. If not for the panic button you had installed in the kitchen, Andy and Ryan might be dead."

She breathes in deep, hoping the air in her lungs is enough to keep her upright.

She caused this.

She lied and told Shane that Andy was sending her messages and she didn't feel safe.

Shane said he'd do anything necessary to protect her. He said there's no problem he can't get rid of.

Her lies to draw out a confession for the murder of Robert Burgess have almost led to the murder of Andy Hayden.

The van speeds forward, drowned in silence.

"Andy was drugged. Now he's been beaten," Davis says. "I ended the tour because I know where his wife will want to be."

"It was the right call, Davis," Michael says.

Johnny looks helplessly at Lauren, her eyes glued to the rearview mirror and Frank's eyes.

"It was the only call," Johnny says.

* * *

A dimly lit cabin on an international flight usually lures travelers to sleep.

But on this charter flight, everyone remains wide awake. They're halfway across the Atlantic, heading to Tampa.

Johnny, Lauren, Michael, Oliver and Doug still wear their concert clothes, now dry from hours of post-show wear.

"I caused this," Lauren mumbles to Johnny, sitting beside her.

"Shane seems to have a *big* problem with Andy," Oliver says.

"I think Shane has a problem with a lot of things," Michael says, turning around in the seat in front of Lauren's. "Shane's tricky, Lauren. I think he's been doing things all along to try to get closer to you."

She looks down. If only they knew how far Shane has gone.

"I know y'all will think I'm crazy," Michael continues, "but I think he rigged those stairs for Max to fall because you and Max were so close."

She nods. "Max and I did everything together. I never paid attention to Shane because I was always with Max."

"I also think Shane struck way back with Cory," Michael says.

"Cory? What do you mean?"

"Think about it," Michael says. "You were in Phoenix and so was Shane. Cory was away in Germany and even Cory said he misjudged how much he drank that night. I swear I think Shane had something to do with Cory getting drunk and messing around with his coworker that night. Cory is a straight-up dude; he never got drunk."

Lauren glances away. Shane had mentioned this too! He told her he wanted to help her but she had left too early the next morning. Did he arrange someone to pop a pill in Cory's drink that long ago? Again and again, everything keeps stacking up against Shane. No wonder Michael's been acting all irritated this entire tour.

"And sorry, but someone's got to say it. I think it's no coincidence that Robert Burgess died and Shane solely inherited Platinum Plate," Michael says. "I know that's a big accusation, but there, I said it."

Lauren can feel Frank's rising nerves, and he's sitting three rows behind her.

"Well, there's an interesting idea," Oliver says. "Shane hating on the Burgess family, killing the dad to get the company, and then rigging the stairs to get the son out of the way."

Lauren can't move, frozen in fear that she'll say something about the FBI's investigation. The fact that Oliver just floated this idea must mean his wife Mary hasn't told him everything. Right now, Lauren needs to steer them off the subject of murder before they decide to become rogue detectives.

"Look, I made a huge mistake," she says. "I should have never started a relationship with Shane. I know my priority is Andy. I've got to get Shane out of my life."

"We all need Shane out of our lives," Michael says. "And we need to do it before he hurts someone else."

"Yeah, I'd prefer not to get fried or something next time I pick up my guitar," Oliver says.

"He probably had someone mess with the frets on mine so my guitars would sound bad," Johnny says. "He's got to go."

"But we can't get rid of him," Michael says. "Shane is still involved. We'll have to finish those shows."

"He's going to come for you, Lauren," Oliver says. "He's probably going nuts because we split Europe with you…and left him behind."

They lapse into silence. The hum of the plane's engines soothes them but they know the calm will not last. The evil they are running from will catch them.

"There is one way to stop this," Doug says.

All heads turn to Doug. He doesn't speak often but when he does, he commands attention.

He moves up the aisle towards Lauren, kneeling down beside her. For the first time, Lauren notices the strikingly beautiful touch of gray in his blue eyes, now looking at her with a mix of sadness and intent.

"It's in the contract. All of our contracts," Doug says.

"What is?" she asks.

"The principal clause," Doug says, raising an eyebrow and looking to Michael.

Michael nods. "That's right. If either of the principals quit, Plebeian ceases to exist."

"The principals have always been you and Johnny," Davis says.

"If any of us quit we get replaced and the band goes on. If you or Johnny quit, there's no band," Oliver says.

"If Plebeian ceases to exist, Shane has no control over any of us," Michael says. "He'd have nothing to do with you, Lauren."

"This would be a legal mess, but we have Todd Peppers representing us now," Davis says. "He's the best lawyer I've ever known. I'm sure he could pull together a specialized legal team to handle this."

Doug remains kneeling, his eyes on Lauren. "We'd save us, and our families, from maybe being next. And right now, family is real important to me."

Oh, Doug. She reaches for his hand, his grip strong from years of drumming. His paternal instincts are strong too, even though his baby hasn't been born yet. Keeping family safe is number one. She must do everything she can to keep Andy and the kids safe.

"The quiet guys are always the smartest," she says.

Lauren slips her other hand into Johnny's.

The droning of the engines and the impact of the moment draw her mind back to an earlier time.

It was a cocktail reception on an early December evening. She didn't want to go, but Cory insisted. The Riverside Resort's Gasparilla ballroom was packed with Tampa's business elite, a crowd that bored her. She found her way to the outside terrace overlooking the river. She just wanted some fresh air. A familiar voice came from behind her; her old boyfriend Johnny. He was on break with the band and had noticed her in the crowd. He asked her if she'd done any singing since college. He had an opportunity. A movie soundtrack he needed to write. Would she want to form a band with him and be the lead singer for six songs? Why not? She'd said.

Lauren snaps out of the memory, squeezing Johnny's and Doug's hands.

Her tears begin to fall. "I never wanted fame; I never really enjoyed being on stage. But I loved every minute I've ever spent with you guys. Even you, Oliver."

She sucks in a deep breath knowing the next words out of her mouth will change her life. "So, I will officially announce…"

"I quit," Johnny blurts. "I quit as lead guitarist. You aren't quitting me."

"What? No, don't do this for me!"

Johnny straightens, "It's over; I quit. Plebeian ends tonight."

The sniffles in the cabin mean Lauren isn't the only one crying.

Oliver nods defiantly. "Stick that in your wallet, Shane Mitchell."

[TWELVE]

"Everyone's at the house, like you wanted," Bill, Lauren's driver, says from behind the wheel of the Tahoe. They are on the last leg of their all-night trip, now only a few miles away from her Tampa home. The night sky has begun to surrender to the morning sun, but sunrise won't fully claim the skies for another hour.

Her SUV looks like a clown car stuffed with people. Davis rides in the third row, talking on the phone. It's midday back in Europe and he has massive cleanup to do. Their publicists, Lynette and Lesley, are managing news of the cancelled tour, while Trent and their tour promoter handle the logistics. Lynette is a few hours behind them heading home; Lesley and Trent remain in Europe.

But news of Plebeian's breakup remains a secret. They've agreed to tell their families first, and together, when they arrive at Lauren's house.

"Tish was making a big breakfast for you guys," Bill says, looking in the rearview mirror for someone—anyone—to smile. "The house smelled real good."

"Everyone is there?" Lauren asks.

"Yeah," Bill says. "Amie and Ashley got in an hour or so ago. Sunny and Mary are there."

"So, they all know, I guess, what happened to Andy and Ryan?"

"Yes," Frank says. "Also, the kids are not home, as you requested."

"I'll talk with the boys and Brittney later tonight," she says.

"And, Andy is upstairs in your bedroom," Frank says. "He and Ryan got back from the Charleston hospital a few hours ago."

Lauren taps the back of Frank's headrest. In minutes, she'll be face to face with Andy. She's not sure what to expect or say. All she knows is Bill is not driving fast enough.

Bill pulls the Tahoe under the portico of Lauren and Andy's home. Lauren pushes Johnny to force him out of the SUV faster.

Their housekeeper, Tish, stands at the front door with her trademark blonde, spiky hair and perky smile. "Welcome home!"

Lauren blows past her, running to the stairs. Each stair feels like ten as she climbs as fast as she can. Waiting at the top is Ryan.

She clutches her stomach at the sight of him. His face is swollen, the left side of his bloated mouth oozing pus, his hands wrapped in bandages. His puffy face opens in a big, wide smile.

"Oh my God, Ryan." She approaches him slowly, opening her arms. "Thank God you're alive."

"I'm good," he says, struggling to return her hug with his bandaged hands.

She pulls back. "First we break your leg in a car accident in Dallas, and now we cause this. You probably wish you had been on duty with the band instead of being assigned to us!"

"You guys are tough people to work for," he says, smiling. "And I'd never want to work for anyone else."

Her smile accepts his very generous compliment.

"Andy's waiting," Ryan says, turning towards the bedroom door.

Last time Lauren walked into her bedroom she carried a knife and a broken heart spilling with vengeance. Now, she's empty-handed and full of regret.

Her hand tingles as she pushes open the door.

Lamps cast a soft champagne glow and the ceiling fan swirls to cool the room. The comforter looks untouched on a bed that is perfectly made; the H pillow murder scene all cleaned up. Her eyes sweep the room towards the sitting area by the windows, where she finds him.

Andy rises from the sofa. Her gut twists. *Oh God.*

Red and black bruises cover his face. His eyes are so swollen, the right one is closed to a squint. Thick bandages wrap one hand and his arms are blue. *My baby.*

A room apart, they stare.

Quick breaths rush into her mouth. And then a smile breaks through her frightened face. "You are the best-looking man I've ever seen in my life!" She runs towards his opening arms.

His embrace swallows her and she buries her tear-stained face in his chest. He squeezes her as tight as his injured arms can.

Don't let him go. Andy tries to peel her off, but she just won't let go.

"Thank God you're safe," he says, tugging Lauren's hair as he strokes it.

She finally pulls back to see his eyes. "Thank God you're alive."

Her shaking fingers reach for his bruised face. She doesn't want to hurt him but she has to touch him. His hands move too, trembling, reaching for her cheeks. His warm hand touches one of side of her face; a soft cotton bandage touches the other.

His quivering lips softly come to hers, tentative, like a first kiss from a young boy. Time seems to freeze as their lips touch. Her eyes squeeze shut when she feels the warmth of his mouth.

Oh God, Andy.

They pull back, eyes on each other.

Their next kiss isn't tentative.

She grabs his head and pulls his face to her.

"Oh my God, you are back to me," he says, kissing her. "You are back to *me!*"

"Completely yours," she says, kissing him. "Always yours."

Their hold on each other is so tight; their lips on each other so damn right.

"I can't believe I'm standing here! With you!" she says, shaking her head.

"I can't believe I'm standing, period."

"There's so much I need to tell you," she says. "So much has happened."

"You think?" he whispers. Their foreheads press together.

Fear and joy race through her body. Her skin vibrates with emotion.

"I never want to move from this spot," she whispers, shaking, her forehead still pressed against his.

He squeezes her to stop her shaking. "I never want to let you out of my sight."

Knocks on the door interrupt them. Johnny peeks in. "You up for company?"

"I'm not leaving him so you better bring everyone up here to our bedroom," she says, squeezing Andy tighter.

In walk Johnny with Amie, Doug with Ashley, Michael with Sunny and Oliver with Mary. Frank, Davis and Ryan follow with their wives.

Lauren's eyes are drawn to Mary, a petite blonde woman Lauren has never really known well. Mary nods to Lauren with a warm smile. The two carry a big secret. Along with Frank, they are the only ones in this room who know Shane is really being investigated for murder.

Ashley and Amie sit on the bed. Everyone else stands around it.

Johnny moves to an open area by a dresser. "There's something we need to say."

Lauren squeezes Andy and then releases him before walking over to Johnny and wrapping her arm around his waist. Michael moves to stand beside her. Oliver and Doug stand by Johnny's other side. They link their arms, just like when they huddle before and after a show. But instead of a circle they stand in a straight line, facing their most important audience: their families.

Andy looks confused; Lauren is already crying.

Johnny clears his throat.

"You never know where life is going to take you, and I was never really sure where this would go. I was just looking for a break; a lucky break. And I got it. I was the luckiest man in the world to have found an old girlfriend, an old drinking buddy, these other two dudes that latched on and some blond kid we've already lost. Together we made the best band in the world."

Johnny lowers his head to refocus his thoughts, and then looks up.

"I never wanted anyone to get hurt. I never wanted anyone to be in danger. I just wanted to make music with these people, and now I can't safely do that."

"No, Johnny…" Andy says.

Johnny straightens. "I've quit the band. There is no more Plebeian."

"Johnny??" Amie cries. Ashley holds on to her sister, sniffling.

"It's the only way, babe. It's the only way to keep us all safe."

Amie scoots from the bed to run to Johnny, just as Lauren lets him go.

Johnny and Amie sniffle in their embrace. Mary and Sunny claim their husbands, and Ashley her boyfriend, as the couples console each other with comforting hugs.

The only woman in the band stands alone, looking at her husband.

"No, Lauren," Andy says. "Don't you guys do this."

She shakes her head. "It's done, Andy. It's already done."

The sweet smell of lavender fills Lauren's shower. Steam rises and fogs the transom windows above the marble wall. Lauren stands under the shower head, lathered in bubbles, her elbows propped on the shower wall so she can hold her exhausted head.

There's nothing quite like the feeling of your own shower.

There's nothing quite like the feeling of being over.

The world tour: over.

Plebeian: over.

Shane Mitchell: over.

Her marriage: hopefully not over.

Her thumbs press her eyebrows while her elbows brace against the marble wall. She stares at the rambling patterns of gray veining in the white marble tiles. The jagged gray lines look like the confused path of her life. Her finger begins to wander, tracing some of them. Some of the veins connect with other tile patterns; they look organized and normal. That's the way her life was before. Other gray veins connect to nothing; their paths stop cold in the middle of the white marble. That's the way her life feels now. Which path is she supposed to be on?

She drops her arms and rolls her head to face the falling water, trying to forget these subtle veining messages. Warm water flows down her eyes, mouth and cheeks.

What an ordeal.

Movement to her left startles her.

Andy is standing there, watching her.

She turns to face him, giving him a full view of her naked body, the water trickling soapy gel from her skin.

What now? Will he want her since she's been with another man? She's hesitant to make the first move after having seen what another woman did to him.

"I'm dirty too," he says with a shaky voice.

"I've got lots of shower gel."

Andy rolls his shoulders, lifting his shirt over his head. Guilt stabs her gut as she sees his body. He lowers his arms, trying to hide his grimace. She glances down, trying to swallow her gasp. His body is horrifyingly bruised, his ribs look blue and the bruises on his arms have already darkened from blue to black. He unwraps the bandage on his hand and steps out of his shorts. His stomach scar from the accident in Dallas is buried under swollen skin. This is much worse than after Dallas. Healing now will probably take longer. He struggled with his recovery back then—what's going to happen now?

Lauren squirts lavender gel into her hand, trying to hide her reaction. She steps aside to give him more access to the warm, falling water.

Even though their shower is equipped with double shower heads, they share one.

Her trembling, gel-covered fingers gently reach for him. Slowly, gently, she massages his chest. *Don't press harder. Don't hurt him.* But it's so damn exciting to have her hands on him again.

He gently cups her shoulders and his touch makes her skin soften like jelly. Slowly his hands move, rearranging the soapy bubbles covering her. Over her shoulders, down her arms, across her chest, then down to her stomach. Her eyes close as he takes her to a mental, soapy, state of peace. The fragrance, Andy's hands, it's so calming.

Eventually, she opens her eyes, the water pouring steadily down her face. She doesn't think his eyes ever closed. They stand inches apart, eye-to-eye, water dripping on their heads.

"I want to know everything he did to you," Andy whispers. "I just don't want to talk about it now."

She nods.

The mountain of decorative pillows is scattered across their bedroom floor; the murder of the H pillow has not been discussed. Their bed sheets wrap them tight, the comforter layering them in warmth. Andy wears a t-shirt and shorts; Lauren a camisole top and shorts. They lie facing each other, sharing one pillow.

Their intimate shower is as far as they will take their intimacy right now.

The soft light of the rising sun is starting to fill their bedroom. Their eyes are busy memorizing each other again. Both of them slowly blink as their bodies demand rest. It's a game now to see who will cave in and fall asleep first.

Lauren wins.

She gently moves stray strands of Andy's brown hair from his sleeping face.

Her love; her husband. Is she really here? At home, with Andy?

A little more than twenty-four hours ago she woke up in the arms of Shane Mitchell, playfully fighting to keep him in bed. She thought she was going to spend the day aimlessly shopping but instead was hit with horrible facts. She turned on her lover; tried to trick him. And instead, the trick turned against Andy. The world tour is over and later today, fans will learn that Plebeian is, too.

Now, she's back in bed, this time with a different man.

She's with Andy.

And she knows Shane isn't going to like this.

[THIRTEEN]

The smell of hickory-smoked bacon lingers in the kitchen. Only rye breadcrumbs are left on Andy's plate from his favorite lunch: Tish's bacon, lettuce and tomato sandwich.

"You take such good care of us," Lauren says, licking her fingers.

"I'm just so glad you're back," Tish says, clearing their plates. "I don't know what's going on, but I figured this is a difficult time. I'll just keep the house running and the food coming."

"And I couldn't ask for better support than that," Lauren says.

"The kids will be here for dinner, right?" Tish asks.

Lauren nods. Once she and Andy tell the kids that Plebeian has disbanded, Lynette will send the public announcement. Lynette should arrive from Europe within the hour.

Davis walks in through the auto courtyard side door.

"Mmmm, bacon," he says. Tish offers a sandwich already made for him. He winks and smiles his thanks to her. "Best BLTs in the country," he says, taking the plate to sit with Andy and Lauren.

"Have you slept at all?" Lauren asks.

"I did, for about three hours," he says. "I left with everyone else at five a.m. and got back here around ten."

"And what's the fallout?"

The side door opens again and Frank arrives.

"BLT, Frank?" Tish asks.

"Sure! I'll take a couple." He joins Andy, Lauren and Davis.

"The magnitude of cancelling the tour is mind-blowing," Davis says. "Deposits lost, tickets refunded, workers out of the last few weeks of a job—I could go on."

"But I couldn't have gone on knowing that Andy was hurt," Lauren says. "You know me so well, Davis. It was a good decision to cancel the rest of the shows."

Davis nods. "I knew which man you really wanted to be with."

Andy reaches to hold Lauren's hand.

The side door opens again. Bill has just dropped off his passenger, fresh from the airport. Though right now, Lynette looks anything but fresh.

"Nice of you to finally show up," Davis teases. Lynette scrunches her brunette hair in an attempt to improve her appearance.

"You try being the publicist containing this freaking disaster that no situation code can describe," Lynette says. "Andy! I'm so glad to see you are okay."

She gently hugs him and sniffs. "Hey, is that bacon?"

"I've got a couple sandwiches coming up for Frank, I'll make you one too," Tish says.

Lynette drags a barstool over to the table to join Andy, Lauren, Davis and Frank. She now sits higher than them, her legs carelessly swinging.

"So, you guys," Lynette says, "I was just wondering if anyone has been drugged, cheated on, injured, impregnated, drunk or fired since I've been on the plane."

Questioning glances pass around the table.

"No…you pretty much got our current events covered," Davis says.

Lauren smiles. They were missing murder, but who is she to add it to their list now?

"So, Lynette," Davis says, "Lauren was just asking what the latest is."

"I've sent Johnny three statements. He'll choose one and I'll send it later tonight after you guys have talked with the kids," she says.

"Shouldn't Plebeian's announcement come from all of us?" Lauren asks.

"It's best coming from Johnny," Lynette says. "After all, he's the one who officially quit."

"I've talked with Todd Peppers," Davis says. "He agrees that legally we are good. Once we make the announcement, he will start the process to sever ties with Platinum Plate. It will get messy. It'll probably go to court and cost time and money but in the end, Plebeian will be severed from Platinum Plate because Plebeian won't exist."

"Johnny falls on the sword and in the end we get what we want: we get away from Platinum Plate," Lynette says.

Andy leans in. "What's the latest from Shane?"

Lauren's stomach drops; she lowers her head at the mention of his name.

"It's ugly," Lynette says.

"And complicated," Davis adds. "He's playing two sides of a coin right now. He's acting like the president of our record company, telling people he's confident we'll be back on tour. But he knows the truth: he's the one that caused us to leave because he's the one who was behind the attack at Kiawah. Shane will be blindsided by the news of Johnny quitting the band."

"And remember, he doesn't know what's happening here," Frank says and Lauren looks up. "He doesn't know if Lauren is back with Andy, if she's upset, if she's being forced to do something she doesn't want to do."

"Mmmm, hold on guys, let me get this," Lynette says, her mouth full of fresh BLT and her hand on her ringing phone. She steps outside by the pool to take her call.

"Look what Lynette has…a cell phone!" Lauren says, turning to Frank. "Wonder when I'm going to get one of those nifty little devices."

"I have one for you right here." He pulls a white smartphone from his pocket. "A brand new phone and number."

"How many times has Shane texted or called her?" Andy asks.

"Enough for me to keep her old phone," Frank says. "Lauren, we have already sent texts to your standby list of friends and family so they have your new number."

She nods. Now Shane has no way to reach her. She has no way to reach him. The strong connection they briefly had to each other has been severed. And it feels…strange. She glances outside at Lynette.

While Andy and Davis's conversation continues, Lauren gets up to go outside. Before she reaches the door, Frank reaches for her arm.

"I took the lipstick," he whispers.

"Crap! I forgot about that!" she whispers back.

"I was able to go through your suitcase and get it out of your purse. I gave it to Mary before she and Oliver left this morning."

"Wow. Good. Thank you. Now we're done, right? Finished with Bruce? No more FBI? It's his case to solve on his own now, right?"

"If we are finished with Shane, then we are finished with Bruce."

"This is impossible not to tell Andy."

"Say nothing. Ever."

She shakes her head. She still doesn't get why she can't tell Andy everything, especially now that her part with the FBI is over.

Lynette ends her call just as Lauren steps outside.

"So, how are you doing?" Lynette asks.

"I should ask you the same," Lauren says. "I'm sorry for all the extra work this has put on you. I know you were already so busy during the tour. I missed having you to hang around with."

"Me too," Lynette says, reaching over to touch Lauren's hand. "Lesley and I were always swamped every time we rolled into a new town."

"So, you were there when we bolted after that last concert. Did you see, I mean, did you happen to notice Shane's reaction?"

"Well, sure, it was easy to notice," Lynette says. "At first he thought the transportation was just messed up, but then he overheard Trent telling the stage crew that they were packing up for good, not just packing up for the next gig. He asked all of us what was going on. He was calling you; texting. He seemed upset and surprised. I'm sure it was all part of his act."

Lauren nods.

Lynette smiles. "Shane's the guy you love to hate right now, isn't he?"

Lauren looks down to the swimming pool, her eyes drawn to the movement of the cool, blue water. The pool's bubbling fountain offers such a calming sound, and right now, so do Lynette's words. "You just nailed it," Lauren says. "I don't think anyone understands what I'm going through right now."

"I was thinking about you on the flight here," Lynette says. "You went all out in your reaction when you saw Andy. And I remember before, watching you after Cory cheated and after Andy…well…went all 'Lauderdale'. You never released your anger back then. I think you said you punched a pillow and had one angry run, but really, you never let that anger go. I don't think what happened with Shane was just a reaction to what you saw in New York City. I think it was a reaction to all of the shock you've had for the last few years. Shane filled a hurt and then suddenly, that hurt was exchanged. You went from hating Andy to hating Shane within an hour. Your head has got to be messed up right now."

Lauren nods. "I'm so angry at Shane yet there's so much unfinished business; so many questions I have for him."

"I understand," Lynette says. "The important thing is not to contact him. Let Davis work on everything through the lawyers. And remember, while we all knew you hooked up with Shane, our fans never did. They still think you are happily ever after with Andy."

"I am happily ever after with Andy," Lauren says.

"I know you will be," Lynette says. "But right now, I think there's something else on your mind."

Lauren looks down.

Lynette smiles. "You can't stop thinking about Shane."

Damn publicists. They always know the truth. She looks back up.

"And I'm not sure what to do about it."

Lynette's phone rings. "I better take this. It's Johnny."

Lauren turns to walk back inside the house. Hand on the door-knob, she notices her reflection in the glass patio door. Her face looks weighted with exhaustion, her cheeks dry, her eyes wide and fright-ened. Lynette saw right through her expression and feelings. Can the others? What if Andy figures out she's still thinking about Shane? She rubs her face with her free hand, stretching her skin with worry. Of all people, she should hate Shane the most! But there's so much doubt. How could someone she's known for so long be this evil? Especially someone who touched her so… *Stop thinking about Shane!*

She lowers her head and steps inside.

"I was just leaving," Davis says. "I have a meeting downtown with Todd. I am confident that in Todd's hands, we will be just fine." Davis smiles and pats Andy's shoulders, which makes Andy grimace. Maybe that was Davis's subtle way to get back at Andy for pushing him into a mirror.

Lynette comes back inside. "I have Johnny's statement. I sent him three and he chose number four, the one he wrote himself. So, what's next for you two?"

Andy and Lauren turn to each other as Frank and Tish look on from the kitchen.

"We get to borrow the kids from our exes for one night tonight, and then the Plebeian announcement is sent," Andy says. "So, I think tomorrow would be a good time to start new with my wife."

He reaches for Lauren's hands and she smiles.

"A surprise vow renewal ceremony?" Lynette asks.

Andy squeezes Lauren's hands. "The only vow I want to make is to get us fixed. And to fix it, I think we should go back to where we fixed it before."

Lauren and Andy say at the same time, "Cabo!"

[FOURTEEN]

Sometimes you get lucky in life. In my life, I certainly have. When you ride on good fortune you should interrupt your trip from time to time to inventory the blessings you have. I'm going to do that now and leave the band Plebeian.

We started this band as five unknowns writing a movie soundtrack and keeping ourselves secret to drive interest in the film. The ride that followed was nothing short of spectacular: an Oscar, among many other awards, three multi-platinum albums, and concerts with fans around the world. I am grateful to the fans that supported us.

I didn't do this alone. By my side were Lauren Logan Hayden, Oliver Brinks, Michael Casper, Doug Maggio and our newbie, Max Burgess. These five are lovers of music and together we made the best. These five are my friends for life.

—Johnny Fulton

Andy leans in to Lauren, the two sitting in the backseat of a towncar. "You might want to put that down and take in this amazing view."

Lauren closes her tablet. "I can't stop reading Johnny's statement. It's unbelievable."

"It is. And the fact that we're back in Cabo San Lucas is unbelievable too."

Andy's right. Time to focus on what she came here to do: work on her marriage.

The narrow, two-lane road twists and turns on the drive to the main resort. Views of the Sea of Cortez peek out from between towering palm trees. Their driver approaches the main resort, but instead of pulling under the arrival plaza he turns into a back area to keep their arrival unnoticed. This private entry plan and their entire stay here has all been carefully choreographed by the capable hands of the hotel manager, Marco Gonzales.

Marco and seven men stand at the loading dock, waiting for them. Frank will take no chances: Marco and his staff have been briefed about the potential threat from Shane, so Andy and Lauren will be heavily guarded. All six of the private bungalows have been reserved, allowing no other guests close to Andy and Lauren's cottage. This will give them privacy, but more importantly, tight security. Shane could be anywhere at any time.

"Mr. and Mrs. Hayden," Marco says, greeting Lauren with a sturdy hug and extending a handshake to Andy. Andy's sunglasses hide his bruised right eye. The cuts on his face are still noticeable, but his long-sleeve shirt covers his other bruises. "Let us go to your room."

Marco leads them through the bungalow cluster and unlocks theirs. This is the same bungalow they had before, with marble floors, a fully stocked kitchen, two bedrooms and an expansive terrace with sea views. He, Andy, Lauren and Frank step inside.

"Everything is secure," Marco says. "With your men and the men I am providing, there will be no unauthorized persons allowed near you."

"You always take good care of us, Marco," Lauren says, turning for another hug.

"The troubles of life can find you, no matter where you are," he says, his eyes lighting up with one of his story-telling journeys. "But the trust from a true love will always keep you safe."

"Magic words, as always," she says, smiling.

"Please enjoy your stay," he says. "And each other." He nods and leaves.

"I'm in the bungalow next door," Frank says. "I know you think I'm overreacting, but I'm going to use the security app and check in with you every few hours."

"I feel better when you do," Lauren says. "That app…it's very helpful."

"Thank you, Frank," Andy says, closing the door behind him.

Lauren takes a few steps inside the suite. "Look, they put both our suitcases in one bedroom this time," she says, smiling.

"I tipped them well," Andy says, smiling back.

Lauren opens the living room glass doors to let the fresh air in. The afternoon is on the cusp of evening, the sun lowering in the sky to yield to the rising moon.

She steps out to the terrace, remembering this space so well. The bistro table and hammock, the two lounge chairs. Last time they were here, her role was different. She was a jilted girlfriend trying to figure out if she wanted, and could forgive, her boyfriend for abandoning her. Now she's the wife who needs to tell her husband everything she did with another man.

Andy joins her on the terrace, standing next to her to take in the view. He's quiet. Too quiet. She's not sure what to say. Usually when Andy walks within eyesight of Lauren she naturally feels pulled to him. Conversation comes easy. Standing beside him now, she feels the attraction, but still feels awkward.

"Let's see what Marco has planned for our dinner," Andy says.

Within twenty minutes of their call, Marco has a seafood dinner delivered. The two sit at the dining room table enjoying wood-fire grilled scallops and shrimp that top their Caesar salads; Marco's choice of a chilled, crisp Chardonnay the perfect wine selection.

"I love the nights on the terrace," Andy says. "Let's go sit out on the chairs."

"How about this time, I'll make the sangria," Lauren says.

While Andy finds two blankets, Lauren rummages through the kitchen for red wine, triple sec and brandy. She pillages a welcome basket for some fruit, and finds some cinnamon from a spice rack to shake on top. She's adding the final garnish to their glasses when she suddenly comes to a chilling stop.

The reality of what she has done is right here, in her own two hands.

She slowly raises her right hand. In it she holds a six inch knife.

She swallows hard.

She slowly raises her left hand. In it she holds a lime.

Oh God, the irony.

She killed a pillow with a knife like this in a vengeful rage against Andy.

She abandoned her marriage in a drunken hunt for limes.

Her hands drop to the counter. She can't even make sangria without being reminded of how stupid she is.

The stiff evening breeze greets Lauren as she carries out the tray of sangria. Andy has spread out a blanket for her on a lounge chair next to him.

Lauren pours two glasses.

"I'll never get tired of this line," she says, offering his drink. She smiles, thinking of the words he once used to get her attention after Plebeian's first concert. "A real friend would have given you a drink by now."

"Looks like an old friend, my beautiful wife, just did," Andy says.

They raise their glasses for the toast.

The soft clink of their glasses and the crashing of waves on the beach below are the only sounds on their private terrace. Lauren knows in a few minutes, the sound will be her voice explaining what happened. She reaches over to the sangria tray to pick something up.

"What's that for?" Andy asks.

Lauren tosses the lime up and catches it. "This is a good place to start."

Wispy sheets of rain wash up against the glass doors of the bungalow. Andy and Lauren's evening on the terrace was cut short by the approaching line of showers.

Side by side, they lie together in bed. Andy sleeps peacefully but Lauren remains awake and restless.

At least she got an invitation to sleep next to him tonight. He could have asked her to sleep in the other bedroom.

Now Andy knows what she did. He knows how she and Shane did it. He knows all that Shane promised her.

Andy will need time to process this. He'll need space.

It's probably good that she didn't tell him *everything*.

She rolls to her left side to face the rain-covered doors. The stormy weather is as agitated as she is right now. She rolls to her back.

Nothing is working.

She rolls to her right side, now facing Andy. She snuggles closer and wraps her arm around his bruised stomach, holding him as tight as she gently can. She's got the man she loves next to her. *Get a grip and fight this!*

Andy is solid in his sleep, exhausted from her story and deep in dreams from his pain medication. He is not aware how Lauren desperately clutches his body.

Ridiculous thoughts flash through her brain. Physical urges pulse through her body. She's fighting a silent battle; an illogical war.

She's not struggling about keeping the FBI's investigation secret.

This struggle is worse.

There was a time of confusion like this before. Back then, it was between her brain and her heart and she likened their differences to ships. Her brain, the logical and loyal one, was like a boring cargo ship and her relationship with her then-husband Cory. Her heart, which was more like a cruise ship with a party on every deck, was the life she wanted, and got, with Andy.

But now her physical needs have entered the war. There's a new ship in her mental harbor. A speedboat that is fast, explosive and thrilling. Traveling on it is dangerous and ill-advised. Yet the ride on it before was so satisfying.

She fights the feeling.

But her body is winning the war.

Her ignition is turned on; her throttle is up.

She's craving a ride on Shane.

[FIFTEEN]

Lauren tightens the laces of her running shoes. Her spandex running shorts and racer-back tank top match the bright flamingo shade of her shoes. She starts to leave for a morning run when Andy wanders into the living room.

"You're up so early," he says, reaching for her. His right eye is swollen from sleep. But he can still use it for a second look at her tight-fitting outfit.

"I thought I would give you a little space," she says, hugging him.

"That's not needed, but thank you. Every second will get a little bit better," he says, squeezing her. "And seeing you in this outfit makes time fly."

Lauren would ditch her run with Frank in a hot second if Andy was ready to make love to her.

"Why don't you stand on the balcony and watch me run down the beach," she says, gently tickling his stomach. "Maybe that will help move the minutes."

She turns to meet Frank at the door.

"I'll have a hot breakfast here when you get back," Andy says.

She smiles, walking backwards out the door. He has no idea how hungry she's getting.

Wet sand grinds under her feet with every pounding step she takes.

Frank and Luis, one of Marco's young security guards, run beside her.

Luis tried to run behind her, until he got a mouthful of sand kicked up from her heels. She's glad he's beside her now; she's enjoying his company.

"Lower your arms a little more," Luis says. "Helps your shoulders relax for the longer runs."

She nods and drops her hands.

"Your thumbs should hit your hip bones," he says. "That's the secret."

"How many marathons have you run?" she asks.

"Five! I love them so much."

"One day…" she pants. "One day I will run one."

"I'll be right with you when you do," Frank says.

Their jog has led them far from Andy's eyes, watching from the bungalow balcony.

"The long runs clear your mind," Luis says. "They challenge you like nothing else can. You forget about your life problems when you run the long runs."

"I'm not sure a long run…" she pants, "…will help me forget my problems."

"Sure it will!" Luis says, the short, fit Mexican barely out of breath. "You forget your problems because the long runs give you new problems, like sore feet."

Frank laughs just as Lauren slows down. She stops and bends over with her hands to her knees.

"Lauren?" Frank asks, bending down.

Her limp body collapses and her butt plops down in the sand. Frank grabs her shoulders while a wide-eyed Luis stands over her.

Breathing heavily, she draws her hands to her face, knees propped up, tears falling.

"Are you okay?" Frank asks.

"I…wish…sore…feet…could…be…my…only…problem," she cries.

Frank pats her shoulders and squats to face her. Luis squats too.

Lauren buries her face in her hands, the sounds of her muffled sniffles all she can hear right now.

"You know what they say…" Luis says.

She heard that. She raises her head.

"…even the sore feet heal over time."

Frank smiles.

Lauren sniffles again. "I doubt time is enough to heal my problems."

"You should still run," Luis says with a broad smile.

"Run away from my problems?"

"Oh no, the problems will still find you. But you run to clear your mind. When your mind is clear, you can fix your problems."

"But I can't run away my bad choices. I can't run from my bad thoughts. Running away doesn't fix my marriage…" Her voice rises and sand flies as her hands flail. "I can't run away and find *another* career as good as the one *I just left behind* and I *certainly* can't run away from the fact that I'm a *horrible friend* because I never bothered to ask someone I've known *for three years* where she worked or what she did!"

Frank and Luis exchange glances.

Luis smiles. "You need many runs."

She smacks the sand and looks at him in disbelief. "I'd need to run a bunch of marathons to clear that much of my mind and I don't know if I can do it."

Her tear-soaked eyes look into his, her body hunched over in defeat.

Luis shakes his head. "Now you sound pathetic."

Frank tries to swallow it but he bursts out laughing. Lauren looks at him and shrugs.

"The young man is right," Frank says. "None of this gets fixed overnight. You're in a marathon. Time, Lauren. You need to give yourself a break and fix this over time."

She shakes her head and cracks a smile. Then she turns to Luis.

"You sound an awful lot like Marco with your good advice."

"Oh, yes. I have many years of listening to him," Luis says. "He's my father."

Her face brightens. "Well, that explains a lot!"

With the help of Frank's tight grip, she stands up. She swats the wet sand off of her shorts, breathes in and looks down the open beach. Ahead of her is a blank slate of sand, waiting for her footprints. Waves wash ashore in no organized pattern, some waves extending their wet reach far and others barely breaking the water line. Looks like those waves don't have their shit together either. Who or what is perfect?

Her problems are far from solved, but at least her breakdown for this hour is over.

"Let's get back to running."

Frank nods, Luis smiles and they continue down the sand.

An hour later, a wet, flamingo-colored mess returns to the bungalow. Moist sand covers her shoes, her body dripping in sweat.

Andy waits on the terrace with breakfast.

"I saw you running this way," Andy says. "The hot pink chick running with two buff guys."

She grabs a kitchen towel to wipe off. "Frank and Luis did a pretty good job keeping up," she says, smirking. "Luis gave me some good advice for running marathons and, well, life in general."

"How do you feel?" Andy asks, pouring her coffee.

"My endorphins are high from the run and my hormones are still raging for you," she blurts.

He smiles and says nothing, the clanking sounds of his stirring spoon the only sound. *How awkward.*

Lauren sits across from him, spreading an English muffin with strawberry jelly. "I'm sorry if I'm pushing you too fast."

"I just need time," Andy says, continuing to swirl his spoon around his coffee cup.

"I understand."

Idiot! Marathons aren't run with the speed of a sprint!

She reaches for more jelly.

The break from the rainy weather is good news for beachgoers below. The sound of a passing boat draws Lauren's attention. Her mouth drops open.

It's a speedboat, throttle up, going fast and reckless.

Her eyes follow the boat as it races past. *Damn.* Riding on it looks so…

She puts her jelly down. These thoughts of Shane have got to go. She gives Andy a sweet smile. "I'm gonna take a shower."

Throughout the day the weather struggles in deciding what to do, just like Andy and Lauren. First it rains, and then the sun comes out. An hour later it pours, then the skies clear.

Somewhere behind tonight's cloudy evening sky is a sunset. And Lauren knows what sunsets mean.

"Last time we were here, Marco told me true love always sees the full color of the sunset, even during cloudy days when there is no color," she says. She sits on the bed with Andy, eating dinner.

She's transformed the second bedroom into a dining room, thanks to her clever internet search of "romantic bedroom dinner ideas" and some supplies from Marco. White, battery-powered candles twinkle throughout the room, gauzy white fabric covers the wooden head-board and rose petals lie scattered on the floor. White pillows in the middle of the bed hold their room-service trays.

"What color of the sunset do you see right now?" Andy asks.

She pushes a few uneaten green beans around her plate. "I see full color but under cloudy skies."

"Me too."

"Andy? Would you tell me if you didn't see full color?"

"I would tell you. Would you tell me?"

She nods.

"Someone did this to us, Lauren."

"I still feel like I did something wrong."

He nods. "I feel like I did too."

"How do we get past this?"

"Time," he says. "I need time to think. I need time to forgive myself."

She shakes her head. "What? You don't have anything to forgive yourself for!"

"I thought another woman was you, Lauren. I opened the door. A woman said she was you. She comes on to me, gets me in bed and I didn't know it wasn't you?"

"You were drugged, Andy! You were half out of your mind!"

"But why didn't my heart tell me? Why didn't I notice? I'm awake enough to have sex but can't even figure out it wasn't you? This proves there's something wrong with me. Once again, I have no control. Just like when this happened before."

"No, no! You just said it a minute ago. Someone did this to us. You didn't do anything wrong!"

Their animated discussion shakes their pillow-top table, shifting their trays. Andy struggles to keep his balanced and seems irritated at continuing to try. He pushes his tray from the pillow and gets off the bed.

"Where are you going?" she snaps, instantly regretting the question.

"I'm walking...to the window... " He slowly points. "Just right over there, okay?"

Her head lowers. *Way to kill a romantic dinner.* She moves her tray and follows him over to the glass terrace doors.

Andy's gaze looks vacant. Lauren looks outside and feels lost too. The view offers nothing to look at tonight. It's dark, cloudy and there's no moon. Rain has made the terrace too wet to enjoy. The soaked rope hammock sags and even the potted plants look sad, their leaves weighted with water.

She moves closer to where she's supposed to be: next to him. Her arm slides around his waist, claiming him again. Luckily, he pulls her closer. *Thank goodness.* He could have pushed her away. She squeezes him and he squeezes her back. Good. She'll take another hug, even though she wishes it was more. Since she came home to him, they've shared hugs and kisses. He even teases and winks. They've been sleeping side by side. So why can't he act like her husband and make love to her? Why can't they get past this faster?

"Baby, I watched what you did," she whispers. "I stood there at the foot of the bed and watched you. If anyone should have known something was wrong, it's me. I should have asked more questions. I should have stayed to learn more. But I ran. I jumped to conclusions and ran. If I had only stayed, none of this would have happened. You can't put the blame solely on yourself."

"It is on me, Lauren. I opened the door and let her in."

"But now that I know what happened, I don't have an issue with what you did."

"But I do. I broke my promise to you. I told you as long as we are together, you will be the last woman I'd ever make love to. I've ruined that promise now. Being under the influence, to me, is no excuse."

She rests her head on his chest, feeling the heavy pulse of his heart. Here she thought this retreat of theirs was going to be about her confession and working through the problems she caused. She had no idea she would be trying to get Andy to stop punishing himself.

God only knows what he would do if he knew that woman was dead.

It's Sunday morning: departure day.

Lauren's grade for their Cabo getaway: A+ on the company and accommodations, F on physical progress. They're not completely fixed but she'll take the C average.

While they wait for Frank and Marco, Lauren's phone comes alive with text messages.

"Looks like we have something to celebrate," she says.

"I'll take some good news. What?"

"Doug proposed to Ashley last night!"

"Wow! You said Ashley is pregnant, right?"

"Yes, and that explains this next text. The wedding is next weekend."

"Next weekend? Fast track!"

"Yeah, so much for my advice to take one thing at a time," she says, smiling at the irony. Who the heck is she to give anyone relationship advice anyway?

Andy opens his arms for a hug. She slides into them and pulls him close.

They're packed and ready to leave this beautiful but rainy paradise. Last time they left together they were fixed. This time, they still have some work to do.

"Young people, new beginnings, tackling their challenges all at once," she says of Doug and Ashley. "Think of all the mistakes they have ahead of them."

Andy squeezes her. "I'm glad I have made my mistakes with you."

"I'm glad I've screwed up with you, too." She looks up at his blushing face and tender smile. "There's just something about you, Andy. No matter how many times I do something stupid, or you do something wrong, I will always find my way back to you."

He backs away, reaching to hold her hands and fiddling with the rings on her left hand.

"These, our wedding rings, are so special, but this," he holds up her right hand, "...this silver ring here...this is everything to me. I thought about this ring every hour we were apart; our promise of until such time. Always, Lauren, it will always be our time."

"D, T, L, A," she whispers about the initials he engraved into his ring after he threw his first ring in the ocean. "I'd like to put those initials in my ring now too," she says. "Don't Throw Love Away. I am never going to make that mistake again."

Their hands move to their faces, his thumbs rubbing her cheeks. His warm touch always feels perfect. He's the love of her life. It's his touch she wants.

In time she will forget the touch she enjoyed from another.

She hopes.

[SIXTEEN]

Massive oak trees dripping with Spanish moss dot the lawn of the Ocala ranch. A nearby lake provides the backdrop for a weathered gazebo, decorated with spools of sheer, white ribbon and mason jars lit with white candles. It's a simple, and perfect, setting for a Sunday wedding.

About one-hundred chairs are set on the lawn, the main aisle decorated with bows of more sheer, white ribbon. No fancy flowers, no expensive décor. This ceremony was quickly planned and is unburdened by stressful details.

The Ocala ranch compound is a short, sixty-minute drive north of Tampa and has been a weekend escape for Ashley's family for years. Ashley and Amie have told many stories about how they'd come here as kids to swim in the lake, play cowboy in the barns and swing from the knotted ropes hanging from the oak trees.

The main family house is surrounded by two guest houses and three barns. One of the barns has been transformed for the reception. A local deli is providing the last-minute catering.

Bill drives the Tahoe with Frank, Lauren and the kids. Andy has sent his regrets. He'd still rather not entertain questions from people who are sure to ask why his face is so bruised.

Johnny stands behind one of the barns, the green lawn now turned into a parking lot. He wears a light gray jacket, khaki dress pants and a white button-down shirt with the skinniest blue tie Lauren has ever seen. She smiles as he reaches to open her door.

"This is beautiful!" Brittney says, getting out of the Tahoe with everyone else unloading behind her. Her floral, high-low skirt doesn't match her blue polka dot shirt which doesn't match her coral wedge slides but she jacked the amazing outfit idea from the cover of a teenage fashion magazine.

Lauren hugs Johnny. "I can see why you and Amie escape here from time to time."

"Perfect day for a wedding too," he says, offering his arm to her.

Lee walks beside them, scanning Johnny's outfit. "Doppelganger," he says, nudging Johnny's arm. Lee's khaki pants, gray sport jacket and white shirt are nearly identical to Johnny's, except the width of Lee's blue tie looks normal. Johnny smiles. "Kid's got good taste."

The warm September breeze softly blows Lauren's mint green sundress, her woven espadrilles the perfect shoes to navigate the uneven lawn.

"Amie's with Ashley?" Lauren asks.

"Yep, and Allison. All the sisters are here," Johnny says.

Lauren nods.

Ashley is the baby of the three sisters, and by far the sweetest. Allison, the oldest from California, can be a bitch like her mother. Amie, the middle sister, is a mix of the two. When Amie is with Ashley, she is a delight, just like when they were on tour. When Amie is influenced by Allison, watch out.

The small gathering of family and friends mingles as Lauren, Johnny and the kids approach the ceremony area. Lauren catches the eyes of the mother-of-the-bride. That woman has never offered anything but a disgusted look to Lauren and she's giving Lauren one of her better ones now. Surely she's upset that Lauren is walking arm-in-arm with her daughter's husband. Lauren squeezes Johnny's arm tighter.

Up near the gazebo are Michael, his wife Sunny and their dancing toddler Simone.

Nearby, Oliver sits on a chair entertaining guests, and especially Simone, with his violin playing.

"Are they paying Oliver for this?" Lauren says, cracking a smile and checking to see if his shirt is inside-out. It looks okay and that's a good sign he's not hung over or drunk. Yet. "Is he that hard up for cash since he's out of work?"

"Gratis," Johnny says. "Oliver is such a charitable guy. So how are you doing since our dreams were crushed?"

"Struggling," she says. "I miss you guys. You took the fall for me, Johnny. How are you?"

"I'm a little lost. It helped to get away for a couple of days. Amie and I headed up to North Carolina to the cabin. I turned off my phone, slept for a few days. How's Andy?"

"In an emotionally weird place right now. We both are."

"You know what today is, right?"

Lauren looks down at the hem of her sundress, blowing in the gentle breeze. She nods. "The tour would have ended today, if we hadn't ended it first."

Johnny nods. "Imagine how excited we would've been to do that final show. We would've been so happy to be heading home. Now look at us: we'd probably do anything to go back and finish it."

"I admit, I miss it. Some of it. Especially making music that makes fans happy."

Johnny looks down.

She smiles. "I loved when we'd first scratch out lyrics on whatever piece of paper we could find. Then Michael would get that look and his fingers would start tapping out a tune and you'd start playing riffs just as Oliver would complain that he didn't like the sound."

He smirks. "The songs Oliver didn't like turned out to be our best."

"Oh, yeah, just like life. You never want what you got and you always want what you don't have."

Lynette interrupts them, arriving with her husband. "What a beautiful day!" she says. "This is so nice; the whole gang is here!"

Davis and his wife walk up behind them, followed by Max and his sister Zoe. Max steps gently in his new walking cast, while Davis walks comfortably in the same pair of blue boat shoes that he's worn his whole adult life.

"The whole gang is here except our army of lawyers," Davis says, his bloodshot eyes showing how worn down he is from the erupting legal battle.

"But at least we have awesome security," Johnny says. Two extra security guys that followed Lauren's SUV now stand near the trees, blending in as obviously as two extra security guys standing near trees.

"Sorry about that," Lauren says. "Until Frank feels I'm safe, I get the extra company."

"When is someone going to tell me what's going on?" Max asks.

Johnny rests his hand on Max's shoulder. "You're not in a band anymore, we're at a wedding and we're trying to have fun. That's what's going on."

Lauren wishes Max knew all the details, but its better that he not know. Lynette's done a good job of keeping Lauren and Shane's brief relationship a secret. Johnny thought it best to spare Max their theories of how Shane was behind the tour's bad luck, including the accident that broke his leg. Max had already lost his father. They want to protect him from more grief.

Max turns to Lauren. "Where's Andy?"

"He couldn't make it," she says. "So that leaves a seat next to me, for you."

Max's blond curls move with the breeze and he smiles. "I'm just happy I got to come."

The opening doors at the main house draw everyone's attention.

Doug steps out, wearing a light gray suit with a white tie. He's followed by his best man, his brother Jason, the band director at Aiden's high school.

"My teachers in suits—lol," Aiden cracks.

Johnny nods his goodbye and takes his seat next to his in-laws. Lauren, Max, his sister and the kids grab seats towards the back just as Doug and his wide smile begin to walk down the aisle. He notices Lauren and reaches for her hand, squeezing her. With his touch comes a flood of memories.

High school orientation night, the night she met Doug. Aiden rushed into the band room, excited to meet new friends. He couldn't resist tapping on a snare drum set up in the middle of the room and soon the band room filled with his unwelcomed loud cadence. Doug walked toward Aiden and smiled. That alone was enough to make Aiden stop.

One time, before a football game, Doug showed her and other band parents how to load the bulky bass drums onto the band trailer and spoke less than twenty words to explain it. At band competitions, first place trophies were always hoisted by his drumline students. And at football games, his students always had the biggest smiles, playing rain or shine. But it was Doug's smile she remembered when Johnny asked her if she knew any drummers for the new band they were forming. You bet she knew one. It was just six songs, so she asked Doug. "Okay!" was the only word he said.

Lauren snaps back to the sounds of Oliver's violin and the feel of Doug's squeezing hand. Smiling, she lets go. Her memories of this quiet, simple man follow him as he walks to the front of the gazebo.

Lauren whispers to the kids, "How many words do you think Doug will say in his vows?"

Aiden smiles. "I don't know, Mom. Maybe less than ten?"

"No, he'll totally max out at twenty," Brittney says.

"Seven," Lee guesses. "For better or for worse; I do."

Ashley steps out of the main house, dressed in a simple, white taffeta dress with white, sparkling ballet flats. Her blonde hair is styled in tight curls and a white sprig of baby's breath is tucked behind her left ear. Amie and Allison follow, wearing pale blue taffeta dresses.

The sisters walk down the aisle to the soft stroke of Oliver's violin, and the ceremony begins.

Lauren hears none of it. Her thoughts have already drifted, her eyes lost in the blowing moss above.

Her life feels like the moss, blowing with no purpose. She can't fight any fights because they are too complicated now. She can't make time go faster to help fix her marriage. She's keeping secrets from her husband that she wishes she could reveal. She'd still rather not talk to anyone she doesn't know. And now she can't even go to a private ranch for a friend's wedding without guards standing like sturdy tree branches watching over her.

She glances down at Aiden's fingers, now counting the words Doug is reciting for his vows. Aiden mouths the final count to her: "Thirty-five!"

Wow! Doug really has come a long way.

An hour later, jazz music from Doug's CD collection fills the converted barn with lively sounds. String lights dangle from the wooden beams and guests sit at rented white tables and chairs. Smiling faces fill the reception. The local deli manager has brought many people to help, pulling out all the stops to help Ashley's family. Doug and Ashley dance together, carefully watching where they step because little Simone is trying to dance with them too.

The dance floor has lured everyone away from Lauren's table. Sitting alone, she watches the kids being silly with Michael, Sunny and...Oliver? Oliver looks like an awkward dancing scarecrow the way he throws his hands in the air. Hopefully he's not drunk. She exhales a heavy sigh.

If Andy were here, his smile would have led her onto the dance floor too. His hands would be on her hips right now; this music would have drawn his eyes to hers. His lips would have followed, softly kissing her, whether or not the song was fast or slow.

But he's not here and it's because of her. Even if he was, he'd be distant. They should be healed by now, but her husband is still not her lover. And the longer this goes on, the more she risks losing him again.

Her shoulder is brushed by someone sitting down next to her. "Amie?"

"I saw you sitting alone," Amie says, her pale blue taffeta dress crunching as she sits. "I figure this has been a hard time for you."

Lauren nods. "Unbelievably hard."

Amie's lips purse as her manicured blue fingernails tap on the white tablecloth. The neckline of her bridesmaid dress is struggling to keep her full-figured chest contained. But nothing is holding back her mouth.

"I thought you and Shane made a great couple."

Lauren gasps.

"I mean, I figured since Andy slept with yet another woman it would be the end of him. And Shane seemed to make you happy. You had your best concert of the tour when you were with Shane."

"Amie?"

"I know I'm being blunt. But do you really think Shane drugged Andy? Because I don't."

Lauren straightens. "I don't think any of us know for sure but…"

"Just be careful, Lauren. You broke up a band and tossed a good man aside for a husband with a dramatic story who has cheated on you before."

Lauren clenches her teeth. "Hold on. There's much more to this dramatic story, Amie."

"I'm sure there is. Frank asked me and Ashley to give you an alibi for a day, so I figured something else is going on. I'm just saying, whatever it is, make sure it's worth it. Because you and Shane were great together."

She smiles with certainty, stands up and moves her hips to the beat of the music as she flirtatiously dances towards a grinning Johnny.

Lauren could cook a steak on her forehead she's so hot. Yeah, she and Shane were great together, except for the chance that she might be found dead one day like Robert Burgess and that slutty woman. *Ridiculous!* She and Andy are great together, not she and Shane! She glances around and sees the likely root of Amie's problem: Allison. The oldest sister stands near the food buffet, giving Lauren a sinister grin. Tall, slender and strawberry-blonde, Allison has always been protective of Amie, fueling her resentment of Lauren in Johnny's life. Even on the night when Johnny and Amie's baby Anna was born, Allison sneered at Lauren at the hospital just hours before Anna died. Allison probably knows all the secrets from their world tour, secrets that Amie should've never repeated. If Allison urged her, it's no surprise that Amie just spit out twisted rubbish like that.

Lauren squeezes her empty punch cup. At least this cup has been good company. She gets up for another drink from the lemonade punch bowl, preferring the bowl on the left which has been generously spiked with whiskey.

Before she refills her cup, she wanders outside the barn to find the bathroom. She doesn't even need to look for Frank. She knows his eyes, and the eyes of the other two security guys, are following her. There's a good chance Allison's nosey eagle-eyes are watching her too.

The compound is a weathered collection of barns and guest houses. Both guest houses are open and Lauren chooses the one closest to the reception barn. Inside is a small living room and a country kitchen. On each side of the living room is a bedroom with a bath.

Lauren walks into one of the bedrooms to use the bathroom. She's close enough to the barn that she can hear the music; hopefully they can't hear her flush.

As soon as she touches up her lipstick, she steps out of the bathroom but notices the bedroom door is now closed. But she didn't close...

A hand slaps over her mouth and her body is pulled back against the bedroom wall.

Oh my God!

Her screams are muffled. Her captor loosens his grip and she squirms around to face him.

Shane?!

Shane's hand presses against her mouth. "It's okay. It's just me. Don't scream, Lauren. Don't scream." He's dressed like one of the deli servers in a white button-down shirt and black pants.

Confused, her knees buckle as her brain becomes clogged with terror. *Fight him? Cooperate? Where's Frank?*

"Are you okay?" he asks, still covering her mouth.

Her mouth has been slapped quiet by a murderer and he wants to know if she's cool with this?

Shane drops his hand but his other hand still holds her waist.

"You're scaring me," Lauren whispers, catching her breath, her body shaking.

"Oh my God, Lauren," Shane says, pulling her in for an embrace. "I've been going crazy without you. What the hell is going on? Why did you leave me? What happened with the band?"

She struggles past the shock to remember what she's supposed to know, while her senses flood with all things Shane: his comfortable smell, the sight of his softly spiked hair. There are things she's not supposed to tell him. Wasn't she pretending to be in love with him? Wasn't she really starting to fall in love? *Who is she supposed to be?*

"It's complicated," she says. "I'm so scared right now." Those words are no lie.

"Oh no, no, please don't be scared," Shane begs. "I had no other way to get to you. I've been trying to talk with you, to help you."

Help her? There's a clue. He doesn't know that she was trying to catch him in a murderous confession. He's not trying to kill her. Yet.

"How did you know I was here? Have you been following me?"

"Someone…I just knew this is where you would be. I had to see you. I want to help you."

"You don't want to be involved with me right now," she says, trying any line of bull to shake him.

"What's going on? I can help you, Lauren! There's no problem I can't fix for you," he insists, gently squeezing her shoulders.

He seems so honest. It's hard to imagine Shane as a man who could kill. She can't fall for this again! She's got to get away from him!

"Shane, you can't fix…" His mouth interrupts her, kissing her with hungry, passionate lips.

Get away! She tries wriggling free but he squeezes tighter and kisses her harder.

No!

His strong hands bind her, the taste of his mouth so familiar. His hands, his lips: *so good.*

She keeps pushing, but each time she pushes she gets weaker and it's not from the physical struggle. She's getting weaker because of the kissing.

She's climbing aboard.

Her ignition is turning.

Throttle up.

Her shoulders melt and her mouth surrenders. She relaxes, pressing against Shane as she vigorously returns his kisses. Oh, the arousing promise of what he'll do next; that feeling of releasing to his complete, glorious and satisfying control. With every kiss his lips pull her deeper to him and now, obedient, she follows. "Shane," she breathes.

"Oh, Lauren." His hands are in her hair, squeezing, and then he moves his hands down to her shoulders. He gently pushes her down on the bed.

Shane follows her down to the comforter, his body pressing against hers. His hand inches up under her sundress, tugging her lace panties down.

She knows she can't do this.

But she has dreamed of this.

Her body crumbles with his touch, feeling his knuckles pulling and tugging under her dress. Waves of want surge through her, fueled by the whiskey-spiked lemonade punch. The room spins. *They are so good together.* She could let Shane do this to her for hours. For days. She *did* let Shane do this to her for hours, for days.

Her brain takes hold.

It doesn't matter how he makes her feel. She has to stop. She's married to Andy! Shane is dangerous! *Stop now!*

"Shane, we can't..."

"Lauren?" Frank screams, pounding on the door. *"Are you in there?"*

"Yes!" she yells, breathless.

Shane shakes his head. "Don't tell him you're with me," he whispers, breathing heavily. "I know Frank's been trying to keep us apart."

If she yells for help that door would be busted down in seconds. Or she can bluff to hide Shane. She looks up at Shane's frightened eyes.

"I'll be right out, Frank!" she yells. "I'm...I'm having some trouble with my dress."

Shane holds still, breathing heavily on top of her, one hand still gripping the side of her lace panties.

"Do you need help?" Frank yells.

"I'm good, just hold on a minute," she yells.

Shane still has her pinned down. "I can't handle being without you," he whispers, letting go of the wad of lace he was holding, moving both hands to hold her face. "Please let me help you with whatever is wrong."

"You can't. It's too complicated," she whispers, wriggling out from under him and scrambling to stand up.

Her dress is wrinkled, her makeup smeared, her hair messed up. She looks like she just got jumped by a madman. She *did* just get jumped by a madman.

"Lauren?" Frank knocks again.

"Geez Frank, hold on!"

Shane moves off the bed. She backs away from him, trying to smooth out her dress.

His eyes look hurt, his arms now empty. He reaches for her again. "Lauren, I love you."

Her eyes fly open. "No, Shane. You shouldn't."

She steps backwards, closer to the safety of the door.

"I'm going to open this door and Frank is on the other side. I'm going to walk out of this room. If you want to show yourself, then stand there. If you don't want Frank to see you, then you better hide."

She grips the doorknob.

"Lauren, please let me know if you need my help. I will do anything for you." He walks to the bathroom and hides behind the door.

She flings opens the bedroom door and Frank falls forward.

"We've been looking all over for you! Why didn't you take some-one with you?"

"Good grief, Frank. I can't even pee in private anymore?"

She knows Shane can hear her. What she doesn't know is why she's lying to Frank to hide him.

She smoothes her dress a final time, and walks away with Frank.

Throttle down.

Ignition off.

Now, keep it off.

[SEVENTEEN]

Whiskey-spiked lemonade punch, to go, wasn't a good idea. Lauren took two cups with her for the ride home after chugging another two before she left. She's spinning a little more than she should be while in the company of her kids. Her nerves are burnt to a crisp knowing what she just did with who she just saw. Her stupid, split-second decision to help hide Shane makes her want to bust out some tequila and hunt for limes when she gets home.

Frank critically scans her during the entire ride.

Bill parks the Tahoe and the kids scramble into the house. Lauren's steps might be a little shaky, but she's walking just fine as she heads for the door.

Frank grabs her arm. "Did something happen at the wedding?"

Crickets chirp in the night air, their chorus now the only sound. She doesn't talk. She stands still, eyes focused on the door ahead.

Frank is on the cusp of busting her. The wrinkles of her dress and her empty punch cups seem to be telling him their side of the story.

"Lauren, I lost sight of you for a few minutes. And you haven't been right since I found you," Frank says, letting go of her arm.

She refuses to look at him.

God, this isn't fair to Frank. He has been exceptionally loyal to her and doesn't deserve this silence.

"You are correct. I am not right. Thank you for noticing, Frank," she says, still not looking at him. "But I need to talk to Andy first."

Lauren bursts inside. Andy rises from the sofa to greet her.

"The kids said the wedding was great!" he says. "You had a good time?"

"You. Me. *Now*," she barks, grabbing his hand.

Lauren tugs Andy's arm as she tows him upstairs.

Her shame is hardening; her focus changing.

She's not crawling in here to confess her embarrassing romp with Shane.

She's going to fix her damn marriage so she's never tempted to do it again.

Lauren pulls Andy inside the bedroom and slams the door.

His eyes narrow. "What happened, Lauren?"

They stand face to face in their dark bedroom, lit only by the faint glow from the swimming pool lights reflected from the lanai below.

"This thing we have going on is over," she says. "*We* get fixed and we get fixed right *now*."

"Lauren?"

"I understand why you needed time. I needed it too. But this oddness has to end. I need you, Andy. I need to be loved. I need to know *you* are the man who wants to love *me*."

"I do love you, Lauren."

"Then there's *no reason* why you shouldn't want to prove it."

"Prove it?"

"Prove it! Be my husband; be my lover!"

Andy holds her shoulders to calm her. "But I broke my promise to you."

Oh God, we're back to this again?

"Can you cut yourself some slack? You were drugged!"

He drops his hands. "I should have known it wasn't you."

"And I should have known not to do it with anyone but you!"

"But you were tricked, Lauren."

"And you were drugged, Andy!"

"But what if *he* was better than *me*?" he blurts.

Her chin rises.

Finally! There it is!

She steps closer. "And what if *she* was better than *me*?" Standing taller, her eyes ignite. "I'll show you right now I'm better than her, if you show me that you are better than him."

His eyebrows rise.

Hers do too.

"Fix us, Andy."

A dose of aggressive Lauren seems to be the perfect medicine. His wide smile must mean she finally got his ignition to turn. After all, cruise ships can go fast too.

He steps towards her and grabs her hands, pulling down so her elbows lock.

Her smile dares him to do more.

His mouth does.

His lips gently brush her cheeks, trailing kisses over her chin, moving towards...*oh God, he's going there*...the bullseye, turn-on spot of her neck that only he has ever found. He presses relentless kisses into her neck, bringing her body to erotic attention while her eyes surrender and close. Suddenly, he stops and stands straight. Her eyes fly open. Then he plants his lips on hers. His tongue sweeps inside her mouth, slowly, ending with a long, lingering kiss. *Whoa!* Again, his tongue sweeps inside her, his lips finishing with another soft, lingering kiss. Her shoulders curl and her knees bend. She's itching to free her hands but he's not letting her go. And his mouth is coming closer again. Flutters engulf her stomach as her body begins to collapse in a state of euphoria when suddenly, he releases her hands. She grabs his shoulders the moment he pushes her onto the bed. *This!* Finally, the weight of Andy's body on hers.

In seconds, his hands are under her dress, grasping her thighs. *These* are the hands she wants under there, and she wants his hands, body and mouth under there right *now.* She wriggles and pulls her dress over her head, throwing it to the ground, while he makes his jeans and shirt disappear.

Wild kissing fills their bedroom with breathless, primal noises; their moans and heavy breathing create intoxicating sounds.

He presses hard on her, giving her what she wants. Still, she pleads for more. "Fix it, Andy!"

"Fixing; fixing!"

Andy explodes, quivering with his release. With a few more pushes of his fixing tool, Lauren does too.

Elated breaths of exhaustion burst from their mouths. Their hearts race, their bodies moist with sudden sweat.

Her fingertips dig into Andy's bare back as she tries to catch her breath. "Fixed!" she whispers in delight.

Andy's breathing slows. "So freaking, amazingly fixed."

Her smile makes it harder to kiss him. She presses her grinning mouth to his, her hand flat against the side of his face. *This is more like it!* This is the love she wants: dominating on demand, but not all the time. Mutual love; the best love: the love of Andy Hayden.

She pinches his cheeks. "Never think you are not good enough," she scolds in a whisper. "Andy, you are the best I've ever had."

Appreciation washes over his face. He begins to move off her, but she squeezes tighter.

"Don't move," she whispers. "Stay like this, right where you are, for as long as you can. I've missed the feeling of you on me."

He nips at her lips and then moves to her cheeks. Finally, his mouth hovers over her ear. "Baby, I'm not going anywhere."

Last night was like a party on every deck and Lauren feels it this morning.

Her husband met, and exceeded, her challenge to fix things, and they enjoyed their evening, midnight and early morning repair jobs together.

Lauren showers early and sees Aiden and Brittney off to school. Lee had already gone back to his dorm last night. Her headache from yesterday's lemonade punch reminds her that she still has to come clean and tell Andy she saw Shane.

She's cooking a batch of cinnamon nut oatmeal when Andy wanders downstairs.

His hands slip around her waist from behind as she stirs the pot on the stove. His head perches on her shoulder.

"What are you *fixing*?" he asks, with a push from behind to emphasize his last word.

You cheese ball.

"Your favorite oatmeal…and I'm adding my favorite *nuts*." She pushes back into him to emphasize her last word.

"Mmmm…I like how you *fix* things." He pushes into her again.

Oh Lord.

"You are making me *nuts*." She pushes back, smiling.

Frank interrupts them, arriving through the side door. His eyes tighten seeing Lauren.

"Morning, guys," Frank says.

"Morning, Frank," Andy says, taking his bowl from Lauren, pinching her waist to make her giggle before walking to the table.

"You've already showered?" Frank asks Lauren.

"Yep, was up early to get the kids out the door."

"Good, I need to see you up in the office, if you have a minute."

Frank's office? Above the garage? Frank never asks her to come up there. She's afraid to ask out loud why. She looks to Andy.

"Go ahead," Andy says, his spoon scraping his bowl. "I've got to take a shower and make a couple calls for work."

She moves her pot off the burner, dragging it over the iron grates. Her empty eyes stare at the pot, looking for answers. If Frank wants to talk about what happened at the wedding last night, she's not sure what she's going to say.

"Be back in a second," she says, leaning down to kiss Andy on her way out.

Their auto courtyard is flanked by two separate, four-car garages. Frank, Tish and Davis all work from the generous space above the front garage. Before Lauren follows Frank up the outside staircase, she notices a work van parked at the edge of their driveway, on the street.

"The cable company?" she asks Frank. "Is Tish having something worked on?"

"No," he says, starting the climb up the stairs. "I am."

Walking into the office space, Lauren comes face to face with the cable guy: Bruce Sanders.

"Bruce?" she says, barely recognizing him without gel in his hair and wearing a hideous pair of beige coveralls with a cable company logo. "How…What are you doing here?"

"Hello, Lauren," Bruce says. "I came for an update."

Lauren walks farther inside, looking around the office. The three of them are the only ones up here. Frank offers her a chair and they sit around a small round table.

"Why the disguise? You could have come to the front door. Andy knows you as Bruce the investor," she says.

"Bruce Sanders, the California investor, wouldn't be at Lauren Hayden's Florida home after her band broke up. You do have paparazzi outside your neighborhood gate."

"Of course. So, what kind of update do you have?" she asks, now noticing a *Kevin* name patch on his chest. So, she calls him Kevin now?

"Actually, I was hoping to get an update from you. I believe there is some information you have."

Panic time. She avoided getting busted by Frank last night. Now this is worse. She's getting busted by the FBI. And she didn't have time to tell Andy she saw Shane! If she tells Bruce, she'll have yet another lie to hide from Andy.

"I'm not sure what you mean," she says.

"Lauren," Bruce begins, "it is not uncommon for someone in your position to have conflicting feelings. You are a victim. You are going to waver between right and wrong; between feeling angry and feeling victimized."

She nods.

"What you have experienced can cloud your judgment, make you do things you normally wouldn't do. You're in survival mode. What I want you to understand is that you are not alone. But I also need you to understand we have a job to do."

She nods again. *This is one of his tricks! He's trying to gain her trust.* Her gut tightens because any second now he's going to ask…

"Lauren, will you please tell me what happened last night between you and Shane Mitchell?"

Frank lowers his shaking head.

Lauren lowers her head too and stares at the top of the table, her straight brown hair covering her face. If only she had screamed for help when Frank knocked on the door, none of this would be happening now.

"You did see him? At the wedding?" Frank asks.

There's no way out of this now. She nods and looks up.

"I didn't know he was there," she says. "I went to the bathroom. I picked the guest house closest to the reception because I knew people were near. I felt safe. When I walked out of the bathroom, the bedroom door was closed. But I had left it open. I had a split second to realize something was wrong before he grabbed me from behind, his hand on my mouth."

"Damn it, Lauren! Did he hurt you?" Frank asks.

She shakes her head. "I told him he was scaring me, that I was afraid. I was trying to remember my story, where he and I last left things."

"What did you say?" Bruce asks, his voice calm and steady, nothing like what he uses when he's in full-blown Bruce Sanders acting mode.

"He wanted to help me. He said he's been trying to make sure I was okay. He wanted to know what happened, why the band broke up. It was clear he thought I was still with him."

"How long was he alone with you?" Frank asks.

"Minutes. Just a few intense minutes."

"I need to know what you told him," Bruce says, repeating the question she just avoided.

"I told him it's complicated. He kept offering to help. He begged me to let him know if I need his help. I told him he doesn't want to be involved with me right now."

"Did he tell you anything else?" Bruce asks.

Lauren nods, pulling her elbows to the table, resting her head in her hands.

"He told me he loved me."

"What did you tell him?" Bruce asks.

"I told him he shouldn't."

"Why didn't you tell Frank?"

"I was too embarrassed."

"It's important for us to know everything you and he did. It helps us understand his mind frame and what his next move might be," Bruce says.

"He kissed me. I tried to push him off but I stopped fighting him. Something inside of me gave in. But Frank saved me," she says, now looking at Frank. "He knocked on the door. I was afraid to yell for help, so I said I was having trouble with my dress to give me time."

"Time? Time for what?" Bruce asks.

"Time to push Shane off me…and get off the bed."

Frank's intake of air seems never-ending.

She looks down at the table again, defeated.

"Lauren," Bruce says. "I don't want you to feel guilty. Even if you felt you might have been a willing participant, you were forced into a situation. That plays into the decision you made at the time to go along with the situation."

"How did you know she had seen Shane?" Frank asks.

"Shane told me."

Lauren's glance snaps back up.

"He called me last night. Remember, I'm still undercover. He told me he had seen you, Lauren. He said that the two of you talked and had made progress. He said he would be meeting you again soon. He is trying to assure me that Plebeian will get back together. Obviously I was immediately concerned about what you might have said."

"I totally understand. I should have told Frank," she says. "But Shane's lying. I don't have a meeting scheduled with him. I don't have any plans to see him again."

"I figured you didn't," Bruce says. "But I was hoping I could change your mind."

"What?"

"Again, we have a good opportunity. Shane has opened a door for us to take him up on his offer."

"Oh no, here we go again. You want me to go back to him so I can get his confession for Robert Burgess's murder."

"Not exactly like before, but yes," Bruce says. "If we arranged a one-time meeting, this could give us the confession we have been looking for."

"No way! I cannot lie to Andy anymore. He and I are just recovering from what Shane did to us. There's no way I can go see Shane again and not let Andy know."

"But if you are successful, then it will all be over," Bruce says.

"And then I still wouldn't be able to tell Andy, right? That's what confidential human sources do, right? They can't go bragging through the streets that they were the source that got someone arrested!"

"You remain the closest person to Shane. He still thinks you are his girl. You are the perfect source."

"I won't do it unless Andy knows."

Bruce shakes his head.

"And I bet I can get Shane's confession now," she says, egging him on. "I'm not in shock anymore. I know who the enemy is. I will play this game much smarter. But I'm not doing anything unless Andy knows."

Bruce's cheeks have a pulsating, throbbing thing going on again.

"Ask for permission. You'll get it," Frank says to Bruce. "Andy is just as important to this as Lauren. These two work well together."

Bruce rises, glaring at them. "I'll be in touch." His coveralls swish as he briskly leaves the office.

Lauren wants to forget what she just heard and who she just saw, although she may never forget the fashionably offensive outfit he was wearing. She'd really like to forget seeing Shane last night too.

"Bruce has now come to my house. Shane grabbed me at the wedding. This nightmare isn't going to end, is it?" she asks Frank.

"It's two murders the FBI is involved with now. And as long as Shane is out there, there could be more."

"What's next?"

"We wait for Bruce's decision. In the meantime, the same rules of engagement apply: you cannot tell Andy about this murder investigation."

"I hate keeping secrets from him!"

"Well, there's one secret you need to share," Frank says. "You better tell Andy what you did last night with Shane."

Lauren drops her shoulders and heads back into the house.

She can hear Andy's voice, coming from his study. She follows the sound, stepping quietly and peers through the cracked door.

Andy sits behind his desk, on a call about someone's investment portfolio. His straight brown hair is still wet from his shower, the almost-healed cuts on his face now shiny with his morning application of prescription gel. She leans her head against the doorjamb, listening, watching.

He abandoned the job he loves to fly across an ocean to find her and convince her he did nothing wrong. He wasn't even back a few days before he was beaten by some thugs. It will be awhile until he heals, a few weeks before he goes back to the office. She smiles, watching him try to be normal, attempting to put this behind him. His only crime was marrying her. And look at the punishment he's suffered. He deserves to know the truth about everything, even if Bruce decides not to bring Andy into this circle.

Her cover is blown when Andy notices her in the doorway. He waves her in, but she politely declines. "I'll be by the pool," she mouths to him. Phone still to his ear, he nods.

For late September in Florida, it's unusually hot. Lauren adjusts their favorite double chaise lounge, dragging it into the shade of palm trees. She doesn't want a tan today; she just wants some fresh air. And a fresh start. She got a great fresh start last night with Andy.

A few minutes later, he joins her.

"Finished what you needed with Frank?" he asks, sliding onto his side of the cushion. He reaches for her hand.

"We have a little bit of unfinished business, but we're good for now," she says, squeezing his hand. "There is something I want to talk to you about, though."

Andy leans his head back, relaxed. "What?"

Big breath in. "Last night, I came home kind of mad."

"I noticed," he says, snuggling her cheek. "It worked for me."

Her nose presses into his wet hair. The smell of his shampooed hair is always so delicious. "Yeah, it worked for me too. But I wanted to tell you why I was so mad."

"I thought we talked about it."

"Part of it. Really, I was mad at myself."

"Why?"

"Because of something I did at the wedding."

He sits up to face her. Feeling his concern, she sits up too.

"Please stay calm while I tell you this," she says. "Last night, I saw Shane."

"*What?*" Andy yells, leaning forward.

There went her nice, calm set up for this fresh start.

"At the *wedding*? He was *there*?"

Lauren nods, squeezing his hand.

"Where the hell was Frank?"

"He didn't know. I had gone to the bathroom. When I came out, Shane grabbed me."

His hands flail. "Shane *grabbed you*?"

"Please, Andy, I need to tell you this without you yelling."

His eyes dart left to right, his breathing rapid.

"I was only with him for a minute. He wanted to help me, to see if I was okay."

Andy shakes his head. "How the hell did he even get near you? And how did you get away from him?"

"Frank saved me. He knocked on the bedroom door of the guest house."

"Bedroom? A bedroom?? The two of you were *alone* in a *bedroom*?"

She grabs his hands again, clutching his fingers, squeezing to calm him down.

"Only for a minute. Andy, he kissed me. And…I kissed him back."

He drops her hands and holds his shaking head.

"Baby, I was lost for sixty seconds, so confused. I know it was stupid. I shouldn't have done it. I should have told someone. I know Shane is dangerous. But by the time I got my head together I was so embarrassed. I didn't know what to do."

He looks back to the house, away from her.

"I'm sorry I caved in to his kissing. I was so mad at myself. I came back angry and just wanted us fixed. I wanted us to be the way we used to be. I was never tempted when everything was right with you."

She lowers her head, shaking it. *That didn't come out right.* Her rocky marriage didn't make her fall into bed with another man. Her stupidity did. *Gee, girl, get a grip!*

His hands twist in a troubled fit, his head still shaking.

She reaches for his hands, holding them, softly stroking the dark bruises on his right hand.

"Andy, it's you. I want you. I don't want Shane."

A shy grin breaks through his angry face.

"He didn't hurt you?"

"No. He scared and confused me, but he didn't hurt me."

"But why didn't you tell me right away?"

"I was embarrassed that I fell into his trap again. I'm sorry I even touched him and that I didn't tell you."

He reaches for her face, stroking her cheek with his thumb.

"We can't keep secrets," he says. "After everything that has happened, you and I can't keep secrets. We can't be 'us' if one of us hides something."

She slowly nods. This is her opening, her chance to come completely clean. She's got to tell Andy everything about the murder investigation, everything about the FBI—now! She knows Frank will be mad. She knows Bruce, or Kevin, or whatever his name is will be pissed. But Andy is her husband; he has to know everything that Shane has done.

Her chin rises as she starts to speak but Andy talks first.

"You came home to me last night. That means everything to me. You could have left with him. You could have done more with him. But you didn't. That's huge."

Tears fill her eyes.

"I want to tell you something," he says.

"I want to tell you something too," she says.

"I want to tell you something first, about a wish I made," he says.

She smiles. "What wish?"

Breath fills his chest. "When I lost you after what I did in Ft. Lauderdale, I had rented that loft apartment in downtown Tampa. The day my things were delivered, I just couldn't deal with it. So many memories stuffed in boxes, all packaged up because of my stupid mistake. Even the smell of the cardboard was making me sick. I wanted fresh air, so I made a drink, and stood on my balcony."

He reaches for her hands, holding them.

"I stood on the balcony, by myself, looking at downtown, the river, the port, the restaurants and buildings. I was so lost. All I could do was pray that somewhere out there, you could find your way back to me. I knew if you ever forgave me and came back to me, for the rest of my life nothing else would ever matter."

He looks back up to her, a soft, forgiving gleam shining from his eyes. "You found your way back to me. Just like back then. Just like last night. You came back to me."

"You are who I want to be with," she says. "And I don't want anything to come between us. Whether we are solid or shaky, I won't make that mistake again. I want to be with you. And I have to tell you something now, too."

Andy pulls back and she tightens her grip. It's now or never.

A chime from an incoming text breaks their stare. She glances down.

It's Frank.

"We can widen the circle. Cable company on the way back now. Come up to my office in fifteen minutes, with Andy."

Relief covers her face.

"What was that?" Andy asks.

"It's the end of all secrets," she says, reaching to stroke Andy's damp hair. "There's somewhere we need to go, and someone we need to see."

Five sets of hands each claim a place at the table in Frank's office. Frank's protective hands are to her right, the bruised, loving hands of Andy to her left. Across from her are the small, folded hands of Mary and the fisted hands of their new cable guy, Bruce. Or is it Kevin?

"That's why we couldn't bring you inside this operation, until now," Bruce says, looking at Andy.

Andy has just been told Bruce Sanders is an FBI agent and Oliver's wife Mary also works for the FBI. He now knows Robert Burgess was murdered and the woman who tricked him into bed is dead. He just learned that Lauren was part of a sting to catch the murderer, and the man who kissed her less than twenty-four hours ago is the prime suspect.

Andy licks his lips, still quiet. Lauren finds his capacity to quickly absorb this much information and still remain upright astounding.

"First," Andy says, "please thank whoever gave permission to tell me all this. I was just starting to develop my own plan on how to deal with Shane after Lauren told me what happened last night."

"Even one person knowing that I am undercover is too many for me," Bruce says. "But we are so close to nailing Shane. We really need Lauren's help."

"They want me to see him again. One more meeting to try to get his confession," she says.

"What do you want to do?"

"Whatever you want me to do."

"I want him arrested and put away. And if I can't be the guy to do it, if you are willing, you should try."

"What happens if he grabs and kisses me again?" she asks Bruce.

"He is less likely to do that if we arrange the meeting in a public place, like a restaurant."

"So, they just walk in a restaurant, table for two, and chat about murder?" Andy asks.

"Not quite. If we arrange it, we choose the restaurant. It would be filled with an appropriate number of our people, so we can control things."

"Lauren is a recognizable figure," Frank says. "This restaurant needs to be all our people to reduce the chance that a fan photo might be taken."

"And this can only be a one-time meeting," Andy says.

"One time and perfectly executed," Frank says.

"She has to be completely prepared and briefed," Andy says.

While they debate her options, Lauren weighs her own decision. Could she really pull this off? Can she face Shane again and not crumble with his touch? But what if it did work this time? Then it would be over. It's *one* dinner, *one* night with Shane and it could be over.

"I want to do it," she says.

The conversation stops. Frank and Andy turn to her.

"I've been walking on eggshells since Clive Winters shot me. I'm scared of strangers, I jump at loud sounds. Now look! I can't even go to the bathroom at my friend's wedding, at a private ranch, even with security people watching me. Somehow he knew I was going to be there. If he could grab me coming out of a bathroom, he could grab me walking out of anywhere. I can't imagine trying to live a normal life knowing Shane might surprise me again."

Andy holds her hand. "Are you sure?"

"What if he sends people to hurt you again? He grabbed me, what if he grabs one of the kids?"

"We have people watching the kids and extra staff here watching us," Andy says.

"And he still got to me! Then look what I did! I was so confused, I helped hide him! We ended Plebeian to cut ties with Shane and he's still coming for me. Maybe this is our last chance to put him away."

She looks to Bruce.

"I'd want a controlled environment. Very controlled. With people around that can watch me. People that can get me the hell out of there the second he tells me what you need."

"We can do that," Bruce says.

"I don't want to talk to Shane to arrange this. I just want to show up, do my thing and get his confession."

"Frank should be the one to discuss arrangements with Shane," Bruce says.

"And this needs to be top secret, just in case someone involved with Plebeian has been telling Shane what is going on."

Mary nods. "I'm concerned about that too, Lauren. It's very

suspicious that Shane knew there would be a wedding, that you were going to be there alone and knew what the servers would be wearing. Rest assured, not even Oliver knows about the murder side of this investigation. He has his theories, but no facts. All Oliver knows is that Andy was drugged."

"Well, I self-reported that to anyone who could hear me when I got to Rome," Andy says.

"I'd also want someplace I'm familiar with," Lauren says.

Andy nods. "A place where I can be too. Nearby, out of sight."

"Knowing you're close would help a lot," she says, perking up.

"Being close enough to beat the hell out of him if needed would be amazing," Andy adds.

"Did you have someplace in mind?" Bruce asks.

"I do. The perfect place," Andy says, smiling. "The Sand Club on Clearwater Beach."

[EIGHTEEN]

Bright morning sunlight fills Lauren's kitchen. A sliver of sun shines across her face, forcing her to squint while she spreads grape jelly on Aiden's sandwich.

"Be sure you have everything for school *and* this weekend!" she yells to Aiden, again.

Panicked thumping from Aiden's room tells her, he's going to forget something.

Brittney joins Lauren behind the counter, leaning in to give her a kiss. "I'll see ya Sunday night," Brittney says, already four departing steps away.

"Have a great day at school and a great weekend with your mom," Lauren says.

Andy intercepts his daughter, grabbing her for a hug.

"Stop, Dad! My hair!"

He hugs her tighter. "Deal with it. It's a dad's job to mess up his daughter's hair before school. Then the boys won't notice you."

Brittney wriggles free and shakes her long, straight brown hair back into place. She straightens her burgundy graphic t-shirt, which doesn't match her blue and green striped leggings, which doesn't match her pink studded purse. But, as always, it works.

Aiden barrels through the kitchen, snatching his brown-bag lunch. "Bye, Mom!"

"Have fun at your dad's this weekend!" she yells back, watching

Aiden high-five Andy on the way to Brittney's car.

The sound of the closing door returns the house to a calm quiet.

If only today could stay this calm.

This is no ordinary Friday. Today is the day Lauren will meet Shane.

Andy slides onto a barstool, looking Lauren over while she straightens up the kitchen.

"Big day today," he whispers, his smoky voice getting her attention.

She leans over the counter, her low-cut tank top and push-up bra offering him an enticing view.

"Could this really be over tonight?" she whispers back.

"Mmmm…" he says, his eyes on her chest. "It depends how bad you want to kill me." His eyes meet hers. "You convince Shane you want me dead and you need his help to do it and you'll have this case wrapped up by dessert."

"I can't wait until dessert."

"Then move up your urge to get rid of me. Get him to prove he's capable of murder by confessing how he killed Robert Burgess and you'll be back to me by appetizers."

His finger reaches over the counter to touch the skin she generously shows. Starting at her neck, he slowly strokes down. Chill bumps pepper her skin; she squeezes her arms to push out more of her chest for his touch.

Erotic touching while discussing faux murder: there's just something about it.

"I've never wanted to kill you so bad in my life," she whispers.

"And I can't wait to hear how Shane's gonna do it," he says, his finger moving up her chest to her chin.

Their eyes lock in another searing stare. All week they've been doing this. Long, flirtatious stares that often lead to satisfying climaxes in whatever room they're in.

Andy's smile leads him around the counter. With no slab of granite between them now, he grabs the belt loops of her jeans, tugging her.

Her body willingly flattens on him. After the feel of his teasing finger, she's ready to do whatever he wants to do to her.

But right now, flirting is all he has time for.

"I've got a surprise coming for you," he whispers, breaking their gaze and relaxing his hold. His smile reeks of mischief.

She wishes his surprise would be taking her right now on this kitchen floor, but she's also curious to find out what he's up to. "You've been working on something with Ryan, haven't you? Where did he take the Tahoe this morning?"

"You noticed?" He looks at his watch. "You only have a few minutes until your surprise is here."

"No hints?" she asks, playfully swatting him.

"Something you need, for tonight. Something I don't think the FBI gave you enough of. It's something to help you get Shane's confession."

"And Ryan had to pick it up?" she asks, baffled.

"I'm doing everything I can to be sure this is over tonight."

She hears two car doors slam in the auto courtyard. Her wide eyes look to see what—or who—Ryan is bringing.

In walk Ryan and the vibrant smile and loosely curled hair of Josh Spencer.

"*Josh?*" Lauren yells.

"Your favorite actor is here for your lessons," Josh says, quickly stepping to her for a hug.

"Oh my God! What a surprise!"

"Andy," Josh says, breaking Lauren's hold to shake Andy's hand.

"Thank you for coming," Andy says.

"You came all the way from California to teach me acting?" Lauren asks.

"That's what Andy asked me to do," Josh says, the two now moving apart. "I hear you have a big business meeting tonight and you need a few tricks."

"Oh, do I ever!"

"Sounds important. And mysterious," Josh says.

"It will be one-on-one and very intense."

"Then I'll get you ready, no problem."

Andy smiles. "I've got to make some calls, so I'm going to leave you two." He turns to Josh. "You're staying through lunch, right?"

"Absolutely," Josh says. "I'd like to leave after lunch for the drive down to see my parents."

"Tish has lunch planned, and she will drive you down to Sarasota," Andy says, stepping away. "The least we can do is roll in a visit with your folks while you're here."

Andy winks at Lauren as he leaves. With every step he takes away from her, her love for him grows. She can't believe he arranged this!

She turns to her visitor. "I can't believe the cutest guy on the planet has come for private lessons."

Josh blushes. "Glad to know I still carry the title, but evidently you live with the greatest husband on the planet."

She nods. "Boy, do I ever."

"This meeting must be very important."

"I wish I could tell you more, but I can't. What I can tell you is there's a lot at stake tonight and Andy's right: I need all the help I can get."

"Then, let's get to work," Josh says. Lauren grabs his arm and leads him to the living room.

They settle on the sofa, Lauren turning to face him.

"You look fantastic," Josh says.

"Aw, thanks. I might have put on a little makeup if I knew the famous Josh Spencer was about to visit this morning but never mind—you're here!"

"I was happy to come when Andy called. I've been wondering how you've been since Plebeian broke up. What happened with the band?"

"It's very complicated, but in the end Johnny just wanted a break."

"Well, out in L.A., your record company president is quite visible, telling everyone, everywhere that you will get back together."

She jolts up straight. "You've seen Shane?"

"Several times. We still frequent the same social circles, even since Robert died."

"I keep forgetting that you and Robert were close," she says. "That's how you and I met, at that dinner at Robert's house!"

"I could never forget that night," he says, smiling. "I've been friends with the Burgess family for years. It was sad to hear Max broke his leg just as you started the tour. I mean, how much bad news can the Burgess family handle?"

Lauren nods.

"First, Robert dies. Then Max breaks his leg. Then Shane loses Plebeian. I mean, I know Shane is not technically in their family, but he's always been like a brother to the Burgesses."

"Really? I never realized Shane was that close to them."

"Robert was his mentor. He hired Shane right out of college and always had him under his wing. He taught Shane everything about the business. They had been close for as long as I can remember. Shane was always with them at their major family events. He was a huge support to Max after Robert died."

Lauren looks to the floor. What changed? Would ambition and greed really make Shane snap and kill his mentor? What kind of creep consoles the son of the man he killed?

Josh leans in to find her eyes. "I know you were close to Shane too."

Her eyes fly open. "Wait. What do you mean? I'm not close to Shane. What have you heard?"

Josh sits back. "Whoa, didn't mean to upset you. I know you've known Shane for years. I thought all of you in the band were close to him."

She relaxes, even though her heart is pounding so hard it's probably vibrating her tank top. Josh doesn't mean any harm. But her racing heart tells her she has to get her feelings for Shane in check, especially before tonight's dinner.

"We all were very close to Shane," she says. "But that's not the case anymore."

"You're not going to tell me what happened, are you?"

She shakes her head.

"But this dinner tonight has something to do with it?"

"This dinner tonight is very important. That's all I can tell you," she says, smiling and patting his knee. She would love to hear more about Josh's history with Shane but really, she'd rather get these free acting lessons. After her reaction a second ago, she realizes she needs to work harder to hide these lingering feelings for Shane. Then when this is all over, she needs to quash these feelings for good.

"So, are you just going to sit there and tell me you are a good actor or are you going to show me what a great actor you are?" she says, smiling.

"Buckle up and learn from the master."

"I'm all set and ready to leave when you are," Tish says to Josh, loading the last plate into the dishwasher.

"That shrimp pita was delicious," Josh says from his seat at the breakfast table.

"Everything Tish makes is delicious," Andy says.

"You sure you can spare her to drive me? Why not Ryan?" Josh asks.

"Ryan will be with me tonight," Andy says. "Tish is just going to take the Tahoe home with her after she drops you off."

"Sounds like you both have big evenings," Josh says, getting up.

"We do, but thanks to you, I sure feel better about mine." Lauren opens her arms wide to give Josh a departing hug. *Cutest best friend on the planet.*

Josh pulls back. "Now, that hug was nice but let me see you cry."

Oh yeah. "Okay folks, watch the *new* master." Big breath in, she opens her eyes wide without blinking. She clamps her lips together, looks down and by the time she looks up, her eyes are wet.

"Awesome!" Josh says. "I doubt you'd need to cry at a dinner meeting but in case you do, you know the trick now!"

"Greatest actor on the planet," Andy says, rubbing her back.

Josh shakes Andy's hand. "You still know how lucky you are, right?"

Andy nods. "Every day."

"Good luck," Josh says, giving Lauren another hug.

He pulls away, walking with Tish towards the door but quickly turns back and points at Lauren.

"Stay in character, use those vocal inflections and emphasize every word at the end of your sentences," he says.

"I couldn't do this without *you*," she says, smiling.

By the time Tish and Josh have walked out the door, Lauren has already slipped into Andy's welcoming arms.

"And I couldn't live without you," she says to Andy, snuggling close.

The hands on the clock have arrived at the magic hour. It's two p.m.

Andy and Lauren stand in the living room, foreheads pressed together in their goodbye.

"You got this," Andy says.

"I'm really going to lay down some crap."

"Lay it thick, baby. Say anything you need to get this done."

"Thank you," she says, pulling her forehead away.

"For what?"

"For Josh."

"I wanted to make sure you had the skills you need to get this done."

"But what you did was bigger than that. You sent Josh, a guy who at one time was a threat to you. That was huge."

"I knew the two of you were good actors. The first time I was in Mexico, waiting for you to come for our retreat, I saw the picture of you two kissing outside that Beverly Hills café. My heart broke because I thought you were a couple. After you told me it was just a prank to throw off the paparazzi, I realized Josh has this acting thing down pat."

"Sending him made all the difference."

"What you learned from him is important."

"Important, like tonight."

"Like tonight," he says.

"I love you, Andy."

"I love you, Lauren," he says, adding a kiss.

Frank and Ryan walk into the room. Frank clears his throat. "Ready, Andy?"

"I'm ready."

Andy squeezes her hands one more time, swings his hair from his face and turns to leave.

"Wait," Lauren says. "Take these with you."

She tugs hard on her left hand to remove her wedding and engagement rings, then pulls on her right hand to remove her silver ring. "I can't try to kill you wearing these."

Andy smiles and takes her rings. "Wow, you *are* mad at me! Nice touch. I'll hold these and give them back to you tonight."

He kisses her again. "I'll be just a courtyard away from you, waiting in our suite. Only one, small hotel wing away from where you will be."

"Knowing you are there is so important to me," she says.

"I'll be able to see the restaurant windows from our room. By the time you get up to our suite, it will all be over."

She nods.

Andy and Ryan leave.

The plan to capture a killer is underway.

And one of Lauren and Andy's trusted friends will help them.

Gregory, the manager of the Sand Club, was notified by the FBI this morning of the sting.

First, he will meet Andy and Ryan on the hotel loading dock. Ryan, who has been told pieces of information on a need-to-know basis, is driving Tish's car so they won't be recognized in one of Lauren's usual vehicles. Gregory will see to it that Andy gets settled in the same suite Andy and Lauren have always enjoyed. This is where they had their first getaway, and where Andy proposed.

Gregory has blocked off the entire downstairs restaurant, Saffron's. Every diner in the restaurant will be a plant from the FBI. They don't want to risk a random fan taking a photo of Lauren with Shane if he's arrested while he's with her. One table near the back of the restaurant, next to eight-foot windows overlooking the beach, will be where they seat Lauren and Shane.

But Saffron's is not where Shane thinks he and Lauren will be dining.

Worried that Shane might bring his own undercover people to scatter throughout Saffron's, Andy has suggested a brilliant plan.

Frank told Shane to meet Lauren at the Sand Club's ninth floor restaurant, Origami Grill. When Shane arrives at Origami, he will be told there was a mistake with the reservation. Origami Grill will be "booked", but a nice table at Saffron's downstairs will be available. Gregory will fall all over himself in apologies on behalf of the hotel, while escorting Shane and Lauren straight into the secure setting at Saffron's. Any hidden thugs of Shane's that may have arrived earlier at Origami's will have nowhere to sit inside Saffron's, even at the bar. The location change will ensure that Shane is alone. No one will be able to block Lauren's escape, especially if for some reason the FBI part of this plan falls apart.

Gregory has also been helpful in another matter. Shane has booked a suite in the hotel, and Gregory made sure the suite was not on the same floor where Andy will be. And while Shane is at dinner, the locks on his suite will "mistakenly" be changed, giving Shane no chance of bringing Lauren back up to his room.

With logistics in place, Lauren has two hours before Frank drives her to the Sand Club.

Trying to relax has been impossible. She paces in the living room, rubbing her neck as she waits for a delivery. The nagging headaches she suffered after the car accident in Dallas have an uncanny way of reappearing at the worst times. While the budding headache fills her head with pain, her brain can't turn off Amie's words. *You and Shane were a great couple.* They were, but in the worst possible way. Tonight is more than trying to get a confession that will prove Amie wrong; Lauren wants the truth.

And if the delivery she's waiting for doesn't come soon, the entire evening has to be cancelled.

Finally, Frank's voice comes over the intercom.

"Lauren, Mary has come through the hut and will be here shortly."

Yes!

Frank's voice continues, "And Oliver is with her."

Nooooo! Lauren presses the confirm button.

Why did Mary bring him? He's not supposed to know about this operation tonight!

By the time Lauren steps into the family room, Frank is walking through the side door with Mary and Oliver.

"Sup," Oliver says.

Lauren quickly looks him over as she always does, making sure his clothes are not inside out. Really though, she doesn't need to do this since his wife is standing next to him.

"You miss me so much you had to come see me?" Lauren asks.

"I needed to grab my Gibson Grabber, pun intended," Oliver says. "I need my Fender too."

Her heart sinks. Slowly, everyone has been taking their instruments from the studio. The fact that Plebeian is not together anymore gives her more motivation to nail Shane tonight.

"I told Oliver I'd like to visit with you too, so I came along," Mary adds, her eye batting in a slight wink from behind her blonde bangs.

Lauren smiles. It's Mary—and what she's carrying—that she needs.

"Take your time in the studio," Lauren says to Oliver. "I never get to visit with Mary." She takes Mary's hand and leads her to the kitchen table.

Oliver saunters out to the poolside studio. Mary and Lauren have a clear view of the studio doors from their breakfast table seats, so they can watch for Oliver's return.

"You ready?" Mary asks.

"I'm ready to get this done."

"Good. Remember, after you tell Shane that you need to get rid of Andy, add a lot of doubt that he really would be able to help you. Say that you doubt a nice guy like him can go so low. Doubting him raises his need to prove he can, that he has before."

"I will."

"This is different than what you tried to do in Rome. In Rome you tried to see how mad Shane would get at Andy and how he'd solve your problem. We thought that would lead him to admit how he's killed before. This time, we are more direct. Now, you arrive mad at Andy and you have the solution: you want to kill him. And you need Shane's help to do it."

Lauren nods.

"In the end, the ticket is you and Plebeian. Make it seem like Andy is in the way of Plebeian getting back together."

"Got it."

Mary reaches into her purse and pulls out a four inch square white box.

"I've been waiting for this!"

"This will go with any little black dress," Mary says, pushing the box to Lauren.

Inside is a black onyx necklace, layered between two strings of smoky-gray, glass jewels.

"This is amazing," Lauren says, holding up the necklace to look it over from all angles.

"Thank you. I helped design it."

"How many listening devices are in here?"

"Just one. Plus a camera."

"Wow—a camera? Perfect! But I don't get a lipstick too?"

"I have a lipstick here," Mary says, opening her purse. "But really, you only need one recording device."

"I'd feel better if this was in my purse too, just in case something happens to the necklace."

"If it makes you feel better, sure." Mary hands over the silver lipstick tube. "But we know what we're doing. One is all you need."

Lauren snatches the lipstick. Even if she had a dozen listening gizmos she still wouldn't feel it's enough.

"Thank you for everything you have done, Mary," Lauren says. "One of the many lessons I've learned from this ordeal is to be a better friend to the people closest to me. I never really knew you before. I never took the time to find out who you are or what you do. I regret that."

"Sweet of you to thank me," Mary says. "But if you had asked me what I did, I probably would have lied to you anyway." She smiles.

Frank comes in the side door.

"I'm sorry to interrupt," Frank says. "Lauren, Cory just came through the hut and will be here in a second."

"Cory? Right now?"

Frank nods. "Aiden forgot his band shoes for the game tonight. Cory needs to pick them up."

"Okay," she says. "Can you grab Aiden's blue backpack? It's probably right by the door in his room and he ran past it this morning."

Frank dashes to Aiden's room.

"Do you mind if I talk with Cory for a minute?" she asks Mary.

"Of course not. You have time, even though his timing sure isn't good."

"Actually," Lauren says, glancing away, "his timing is perfect."

She walks to the front door to meet him but he's already standing in the foyer, tucking his keys in his pocket. But she thought the front door was locked. Note to self: Cory's key still unlocks the house. She might want to look into that.

"Hey there," Lauren teeters on her toes to give him a quick hug. Frank and Mary walk into the foyer and Frank hands him Aiden's backpack.

"Thanks," Cory says. "Oh, hi Mary." Mary nods.

"Thanks for picking this up for Aiden," Lauren says, pointing to the backpack. "He had a hectic morning."

"You won't be at the football game tonight, right?" Cory asks.

"No, I have a dinner meeting tonight. Do you have a second to talk?"

"Um, sure."

Lauren excuses them and leads him into the living room. His blue eyes look gracious but curious as he scans the room. It's been a while since they've talked face to face. She gestures for him to sit, and then chooses a chair across from him.

"So you'll be at the game with Val tonight?" she asks.

"Yes."

"You've been dating her for, what, six months now?" she asks, smiling. He nods.

"I'm happy for you," she says, looking down.

Every molecule in the room feels bloated in awkwardness. She's really not interested in her ex-husband's love life. She steadies herself with a big breath and launches into a topic they have never discussed.

"I wanted to ask you something, from a few years ago."

Cory's face screams indifference, his feet already tapping the floor. She won't have long before he says he has something more important to do, so she'd better hurry.

"I wanted to ask you…about what happened in Germany."

"Germany?" Cory asks, his head tilted.

"Yes, Germany. Back when you and I, well. I'm sorry to bring this back up, but I was curious about something."

Cory swallows. His feet still.

"That night you got drunk, and…well…I was wondering what you were drinking that night."

She might as well be wearing two noses the way he is looking at her right now.

"What…like what type of drink?" Cory asks, confused.

She nods. "Yeah. You don't normally drink. Everyone knows that. So it was strange, you know, that you were drunk."

"Why are you asking me this?"

She looks down. "I really can't tell you why. But it is important for me to know."

"I was drinking rum and Coke. I had one or two. Look, I don't think I need to explain any of this now."

"Oh, I'm not trying to blame you or anything, really. But that night, you said you felt *really* drunk, right?"

His feet shift back and forth. "I felt drunk, and alive."

She grits her teeth. She isn't looking for a fight. She's looking to prove Michael's theory that Cory was drugged, that long ago. Amie's mantra that '*Shane is so perfect*' keeps ringing in her head, giving her lingering doubts that Shane could have been behind any of this.

"We all know how alive you were, Cory. I saw the pictures," she says. "I was just trying to…" Her ringing phone interrupts them. She glances to her phone but Cory has already noticed the caller ID.

"Johnny," he says. "It's always Johnny."

She sends the call to voicemail but it's too late. Cory is on his feet, heading towards the door.

"Listen, I'd love to talk more about my drinking habits but I've got to get this backpack to Aiden. Val and I have tonight covered. You and Andy can go to next week's game."

Lauren nods. "Hey, I know my questions seem weird, but I just needed to know."

Cory stops before stepping out of the living room. "We're in a good place now. Don't mess it up by poking around the past. It doesn't matter how much I drank. You and I weren't going to make it."

No! That's not why she's asking these questions! She knows they weren't going to make it. Her lawyer was drawing up divorce papers before he even drank his first rum and Coke in Germany. *Ugh!*

"Have fun at the game," she says. Cory pinches his lips and leaves.

She stands alone, her head tipped back, eyes on the ceiling. She probably shouldn't have asked him that. He must think she's nuts. But is Michael's theory right? Do two rum and Cokes make a man "misjudge" how much he drank? Can't a normal man handle two drinks? Or was Cory really drugged and Shane the one behind it, that long ago?

She shakes her head. Why is she even bothering to investigate this? Everything points to Shane, so why can't she get on board? Now she's acting just like she did on the world tour when she set out to prove popping guitar frets and faulty cables had nothing to do with them being in danger. She's not a detective. Let it go!

Her phone chimes with a new voicemail message alert, at the same time it rings again.

Johnny? Calling again? Why?

This time, she answers.

"Hey," Johnny says. "How are you?"

"Fine. I saw you called. Sorry, I was talking to Cory and couldn't answer."

"Yeah, what are you doing tonight?"

"I'm having dinner with someone. Why?"

"Oliver just called me. Told me he was at your place."

"He's in the studio, picking up two of his guitars."

"I was thinking of coming over to see you."

"Not a good night."

"I've just been thinking a lot. About the band and stuff."

She has no emotional energy for Johnny right now. And this is so unusual for him to call twice in one minute.

"Tomorrow is a better day. Much better."

Quiet fills their call. *Um...hello?*

"I still feel so betrayed," Johnny blurts. "Shane had been like one of us."

She closes her eyes. She's hours away from hopefully getting Shane's confession. By the end of the night, Shane should be arrested. But she can't tell Johnny!

"It's embarrassing," she says, playing along. "It makes you feel like you have no sense of right and wrong. You get close to someone only to realize they may not be the person you thought they were."

"You just need to forget how close you had gotten to Shane."

She quiets. Funny, his wife seems so on board with team Shane and Lauren that she'd probably plan their wedding if asked. But Johnny wants her to erase every memory?

"Lauren?"

"I'm not sure I'm ever going to forget how close I had gotten to Shane," she blurts.

Johnny's silence confirms she probably shouldn't have said that to an ex-boyfriend, especially one who has always been interested in her personal life.

"You haven't talked with Shane, right?" Johnny asks.

"Only Davis has, through lawyers," she lies.

"Good. You really shouldn't."

"Hey, look, I need to run," she says, trying to end the rambling call.

"Call you tomorrow. Enjoy your dinner tonight."

Hearing his words makes her close her eyes. Tonight's dinner will be anything but enjoyable but it could pay off for him. If she's successful at getting rid of Shane, Johnny could get his dream back.

Lauren ends the call and rejoins Mary. Oliver has come in from the studio, entertaining himself at the breakfast table by gnawing a cigar and leaning his chair back on two legs. She bathes him in an up-and-down gaze as she takes her seat.

"What are you staring at?" Oliver asks.

"I'd like for you to put all four chair legs on the floor, for starters," she says. Oliver leans forward, the front two legs of the chair hitting the floor with a thud. He's worse than her kids.

Lauren smiles. "And I'm glad to see you are pulled together. You know, I was starting to worry about you on tour. You seemed to be getting, well, lost."

He looks at Mary, then back to Lauren.

"I was a little lost," he says.

"But you weren't drinking the night I came back to Rome. The night you told me I shouldn't drink."

Oliver nods and looks again to Mary.

"When Mary called and told me how you found Andy, I knew this was going to be rough. No one in Rome knew you were coming in hot. I figured Frank would have his hands full."

"I gave you purpose, didn't I?"

"You gave me a fit. And yes, your problem gave me something to do other than drink."

"Have you stopped drinking?"

"Matter of fact, I haven't had a drink since you toasted me like a sorority sister in Rome. So fuck you, here's to me."

Mary smiles. "Well, actually…you did have a little to drink at Doug's wedding."

Oliver shrugs. "I didn't know the bowl on the left had whiskey." He turns to Lauren. "Did you try that stuff?"

She laughs. "Yeah, a couple cups. It helped me get through a very difficult night."

"Well, I don't have to drink to get through anything anymore," Oliver says, putting his wet, chewed cigar on the table. Lauren looks at the disgusting, moist wad that was just in his mouth. Seriously, this guy is worse than a kid.

"Glad to hear that," Lauren says. "I'm glad you kept things legal too." Oliver still doesn't know that the guy he partied with works for the FBI. If he had been caught using drugs, he'd have to explain that to his FBI wife.

Mary nods and points to the kitchen clock. "I hate to cut our conversation short but I know you've got to go."

Lauren turns to the clock, nerves warming her body when she sees the time. It's time to get serious now.

Mary smiles. "Good luck at dinner, Lauren."

[NINETEEN]

Killer car: check.

Killer dress: check.

Killer hair, makeup and body: as best she can, check.

Ready to catch a killer? Check.

The sting is set and Lauren is on the way. Frank drives her new, white Porsche Panamera Turbo S Executive over the causeway on this beautiful, sunny September evening. With only one block to go until they reach the brick-lined driveway of the Sand Club hotel, they get caught.

By a traffic light.

Lauren's cherry-red polished fingernails tap her seat.

She can see the rooftop of the Sand Club ahead, its colorful flags waving in the Gulf breeze.

"You're in range now," Frank says.

"They can hear me?"

Frank nods.

Her necklace and lipstick are live to the surveillance team monitoring her.

Frank pulls up to the valet and a familiar man reaches for her door. It's the same man who was standing in the elevator in Rome, who scanned her purse for listening devices. Even the valets tonight work for the FBI.

She gives him a pleasant smile and steps out of the car. The sharp heels of her Louis Vuitton black patent pumps sound as if they're slicing the ground she walks on. She's opted to show the soft, spray-tanned skin of her bare legs instead of hiding behind a pair of pantyhose. Behind her ears and on each wrist is a generous dose of the perfume that drives Shane crazy. Her short, black lace dress with long sleeves has a nice surprise for Shane the first time she turns: a revealing open back.

With every step of her clicking heels she feels empowered. She squeezes her Prada clutch so hard she's probably bent the lipstick recorder inside. With Frank by her side they walk with purpose through the lobby. In seconds they reach the elevators, heading to the Origami Grill on the ninth floor.

The elevator doors close, leaving Frank and Lauren alone in a rising cab that feels weighted with nervous air. Lauren stares straight ahead and Frank does the same. *Just breathe.*

The elevator arrives on the ninth floor and they walk down the long hallway in a stroll that feels endless. She begins to smell the delicious food and knows the end of her walk is near. Shane is near. The reason Plebeian had to cancel a world tour and end Johnny's dream is near.

She turns to make her arrival, walking right towards his smile, his slightly spiked hair, his brown eyes.

Her eyes light up in a practiced greeting.

"Shane," she says, reaching for a welcome hug. His fitted black sport coat parts as he opens his arms to her, a white dress shirt and no tie underneath.

"Lauren." He reaches for a hug. The feel of his warm hands on her back tells her he just discovered the open back of her dress.

Their greeting is fit for public view, their relationship still a secret to fans. That is, the relationship Shane thinks he still has with Lauren.

Pulling back, their eyes dart in heavy, teasing glances.

His teasing glances seem real. Hers are well-rehearsed.

"I can't believe you're here," Shane whispers in her ear. She's pretty sure her onyx necklace heard that.

"Thank you for meeting me here. I love this place," she says. "I have so much I need to tell you. So much I couldn't tell you at the wedding. I hope you don't mind a long dinner tonight."

"I'm ready to take this into morning. But first, we may have to sit at the bar for a while. There's a problem with the reservation," he whispers, just as Gregory notices Lauren.

"Lauren! Good evening! What a pleasant surprise," Gregory says, greeting her with a hug and a perfectly executed lie.

"I'm dining with Shane Mitchell, the president of our record company. Well, our former…well, it's complicated. We have a business meeting tonight."

"I just came up to assist with Mr. Mitchell's reservation," Gregory says. Glancing down at the hostess's computer, his hands rise to his face. "I believe we have made a mistake. It seems a large group will be dining here at Origami tonight, and a few existing reservations were mistakenly deleted. But I can seat you immediately downstairs in Saffron's."

"I love Saffron's too! Is that okay with you, Shane?"

He hasn't taken his eyes off her since their hug. "We can have burgers at the outside bar, doesn't matter to me."

"Then allow me to escort you," Gregory says. "Um, escort you to Saffron's, Mr. Mitchell. Not the poolside bar."

They share a laugh and turn to leave, Frank following behind them.

Shane glides his hand to Lauren's bare back as they walk down the long ninth floor hallway. His touch might look friendly, but it sears her skin. She glances to the right, out the windows that face the hotel's center courtyard. She can see her suite at the end of the next wing. Andy is waiting for her, *right there.*

Curiosity is killing her; she's dying to turn around to see if anyone is following them. Shane's people—if brought any—would be scrambling to follow them. *What's happening behind her?*

Gregory launches into their scripted conversation as they wait for the elevator. "How's Andy?" he asks.

Lauren looks down. "He's busy working on a project right now and I really don't know how he is."

Gregory acts surprised. The elevator opens and Lauren leads Shane in, offering him a view of her open-back dress. Smiling, Shane moves to the back of the elevator. Lauren stands in front of him. More view.

"How have you been, Frank?" Gregory asks, and the two fill the descending elevator ride with meaningless conversation.

It's time to turn things up. She's close enough to Shane to lean back and push her hips into him. He presses back. That will help motivate him to give her the information she wants, even though she feels like a slut doing it.

The elevator arrives on the first floor and the group begins their walk to Saffron's.

"So, Andy still lives in your home?" Shane quietly asks, walking beside Lauren.

"He's under my roof, not in my bed."

"Does he know you're meeting me?"

"No, and I don't care if he finds out. That's one of the reasons I wanted to meet you in a public place. I don't care if a photo gets taken of us, and actually, it might help spread rumors that Plebeian could be getting back together. I believe Andy would find both of those rumors irritating."

Shane nods.

Their group arrives under the modern yellow and black script sign of Saffron's. Gregory approaches the hostess stand.

"This is the Mitchell party from Origami. Please treat them as my guests. A nice table, maybe number twenty-four by the window, if it's available," Gregory says.

"Of course. Please follow me," the hostess says, gathering menus.

"I'll be at the bar," Frank says to Lauren.

Shane stops. "Frank, I wanted to thank you."

"Thank me? What for?"

"I'm not sure what has happened, and maybe tonight I'll know more, but I knew when I was apart from Lauren that you would be watching her. I appreciate you keeping an eye on her these last few weeks since I was unable to."

Frank stiffens.

Shane again places his hand on Lauren's open back.

She's really uncomfortable with his hand but very comfortable in this restaurant. Everyone she sees is part of the plan. Several couples are seated at tables, even a dressed up family is finishing their dinner. They've done a nice job mixing young couples with older ones, and staggering the stages of their meals.

They are led to a table by a large window. Their view overlooks the white sand beach and the end of a beautiful sunset. The table is set with two candles and a small vase with three roses. Maybe they hold listening devices too.

They take their seats.

Lauren exhales a relieved breath. *Made it.* It's in her hands now. Drive this conversation, get his confession and get the hell out of here.

Shane leans towards her. "I'm so mad I don't know whether to hold you in my arms or take you up to my suite and spank you."

Holy aggressive start!

Lauren opens her napkin with a forceful snap. "That's too bad you are considering them as an either-or. I may have wanted them both." She slaps the napkin on her lap.

A waiter approaches for their drink orders. Shane nods for Lauren to order first.

She looks at Shane, not the waiter.

"I'd like a shot of tequila. Extra limes," she snaps.

"I'll take the same. Two shots," Shane says, his eyes squarely on her.

This is a little tenser than she imagined.

As soon as the waiter walks away, she leans in. "I've got a problem, I've asked you to meet with me for help and you want to spank me?"

"Lauren, I am so frustrated right now I'm not sure what to do next."

"Well, let me give you a hint: getting hit by a guy is not my favorite thing," she whispers. "I'm not crazy about guys who grab me outside of bathrooms either."

He leans closer with flaring eyes. "The biggest band on my label just quit in the middle of a world tour and took the woman I love with them. I don't know if you are safe, if you are in danger, if you are happy or sad. You didn't call or text. I got nothing from you, Lauren. Nothing."

She sits back. She better dial this down and get back into character as the helpless, needy woman who needs to kill her husband.

She slides her elbows on the table, resting her chin on her fingers and closing her eyes to feign frustration. "I can't imagine what this has done to you. I'm so sorry," she whispers. "It's been so hard to not contact you but I didn't want to get you involved. Everything is such a mess."

"Can we start at the beginning? Why did Plebeian leave in the middle of the tour?"

"Because of Andy."

Shane sits straighter. Since he's the one who called in the hit to beat Andy, this shouldn't be news to him. But right now, he's acting pretty well.

"Andy has gotten involved with some strange people."

"Like the woman he had sex with at The Burberry hotel?"

Rude. "That's one of them. He's had some investments go bad for some clients. He's used my money to try to fix his problems. There have been threats, strange visits, he even got beat up in a fist-fight with some people. It's a mess right now. I had to make sure the kids were okay."

"But Johnny is the one who quit. Why?"

"Johnny took the fall for me. My life is unraveling and Andy's pulling the string. There's no way I could have finished the tour."

"I don't want you around that danger. Why don't you leave Andy?"

"I can't; the kids. Look, my boys' lives were upended when their father cheated on me. Then I pieced together our family after Andy left me. I convinced the boys that I made the right decision taking Andy back. I'll be a complete failure in their eyes if I leave Andy now."

"If you won't leave Andy then that leaves no future for you and me. I don't like that."

The waiter arrives with their tequila shots.

"Would you be interested in ordering any appetizers?" the waiter asks.

Shane shakes his head. "We're in no hurry tonight. Please, not now." The waiter leaves.

Thank goodness Shane doesn't want to eat. Looking at food while she's trying to talk about killing Andy might make her puke.

Lauren picks up her shot glass. He mirrors her.

"Shots like this brought us together," she says. Her foot has found the inside of his leg and she gently rubs him.

"Do you still wanna play?" he asks.

She smiles. "I want a new life. I want to be free. And if I'm free, I can play with you all day and all night." Her foot continues to rub inside his leg.

"Then here's to the start of a new life."

They both toss back a shot and bite a lime.

"I don't have Davis here to throw this at." She laughs.

"And we both forgot to start with the salt," he says.

"We can't do anything right, can we?"

"No, Lauren, we can do everything right, together. We can have the life I've dreamed of. I just need to get you back, and Plebeian."

She shakes her head. "There will be no Plebeian as long as Andy's around."

"What do you mean?"

"He sold all the equipment in our home studio, for starters. He's had huge fights with Johnny and Oliver. Everyone is now mad at each other."

"This is getting ridiculous. Andy is unhinged. You've gotta get rid of this guy."

She looks down at Shane's extra shot.

"One shot but two of us." She lowers her chin, adding a seductive stare.

"That could be a problem."

"How about you help me get rid of my husband and I'll let you have that shot."

Shane pushes the drink to the center of the table.

"What? My offer's not good enough?"

"Oh, I want to help you get rid of your husband. But I'd like more than one drink to do it."

She smiles, her foot still pressing the inside of Shane's leg.

"You said you can solve any problem and I need help, Shane. That's why I wanted to see you tonight. I need help with this. I've got to get rid of Andy but make it look clean to the kids. I've never done anything like this before. I never dreamed I would need to ask it. Maybe you know people who can help me. Or maybe, you can help. I'm desperate."

"I want to take care of you. I will handle this."

"If you help me, I'll give you more than this one drink." She nudges the shot back to him.

"I've gotten rid of problems bigger than a husband before. But what else is on the table for me?"

Lauren smiles and looks out to the beach view. *This is going so well! Don't screw it up.* She pulls her stare back inside to look at Shane.

"Tell me how you can do it."

"Tell me what I get."

"This conversation is too good to be true. You really can help me with this? How?"

"There are drugs. Drugs that can make people do crazy, and some-times fatal, things."

"Have you used them before?"

"I'm not going to tell you until you tell me what I get first," he says, eyes smoldering.

Her chest throbs in a nervous pounding. She's getting light-headed keeping track of what he's saying. The agents aren't moving to arrest him, so she hasn't gotten enough information yet. She has to keep teasing and pressing Shane.

"It sounds like you are experienced, and for that, you should get a big payout."

"I'm waiting to hear the plan."

"Free me from Andy and then I'm all yours."

Shane softly bites his lip. "I thought you were already mine."

Ugh. Sweeten this offer. "Get rid of Andy for good and I'll bring back Plebeian."

"This is too easy a task for such an incredible payout." He smiles wickedly.

"Easy? Getting rid of someone like Andy is easy? How?" she asks, squirming in her chair.

"It's easy to get rid of something you don't want."

"By using the drugs you have?"

"Easy."

"You've used them before?"

"Easily."

"Shane! I didn't realize you were so dangerous," she says, tracing her finger around the lip of the shot glass.

"And I never knew you were up for danger. There's a dark side to everyone, Lauren."

"How do I know we wouldn't get caught?"

"There's ways around that too."

"You're telling me nothing." She stretches one hand across the table, reaching for his. His eyes open wider.

"You're touching my hand, in public? Are you ready to show the world that you are mine?"

Yep, ready to show all the agents in this room.

Her other hand moves forward, fingers walking towards him in a gentle, teasing crawl. Her hands now completely cover his. She squeezes. He smiles triumphantly and squeezes back.

"You just told me you will free my life by getting rid of my husband. Holding your hand is just the beginning of what I hope to do with you. But I still have so many questions. If you did this before, how did you not get caught?"

Shane tightens his grip.

"Lauren, we have one little thing between us: Andy. One little thing and then our future begins and Plebeian can return. I'm not worried about the details."

"I *am* worried about the details! I don't know why you won't tell me."

"You've got nothing left to offer me, that's why! I've got this one shot to drink, I've already got you and you've agreed to give me Plebeian. I don't have to tell you anything unless you have something more to offer."

Shane smiles with such excitement, such devious excitement. He's just offered to kill Andy, and he wants Lauren to promise some type of play payment before giving her more information. He may be physically attractive but right now he's looking like a sick, sick man.

"I think you're shooting blanks," she says. "You've got a blank resume. You've never done anything like this before. You're trying to convince me you'll fix my problem and you've never knocked off anyone before."

"Are you really being serious?"

"Name names. Give me one name of someone you have knocked off before or I seriously have to get help elsewhere."

"I'll give you a name if you give me something in return."

She leans forward, squeezing his hand. "You are completely irresistible and you are driving me crazy with this teasing game."

"Driving you crazy? Like how I made you wait for breakfast in Lido di Ostia?"

Shane's smile right now would make a normal girl strip off her clothes and jump over the table to have him. But Lauren's not a normal girl anymore. He's not affecting her the way he used too. He's making her disgusted.

"This is much worse than your revenge for a stolen towel. I'm asking for references to be sure a job will get done and you are demanding payment before I get my references."

"I'm not demanding payment. I'm demanding to know what my payment will be."

Ugh! Going round and round in these verbal circles is getting ridiculous. Even the agents listening must be getting bored. Andy's probably pounding the table in the suite upstairs, yelling for her to move faster. She's got to heat things up. She's got to think of something that will crack him!

She pulls back her hands which draws Shane's concerned eyes. She lowers her chin and looks at him with her best bedroom eyes.

She just thought of the perfect thing to offer.

"Prove to me that you've knocked off someone by giving me one name. One name to prove you are the man I think you are. Then, I'll prove to you I'm yours."

"How?"

"Take me up to your room, and spank me."

He jolts straight, his eyes wide.

She gently bites her lower lip, waiting to add the magic word.

"Please," she whispers.

His chin rises. "Robert Burgess."

Her eyes fly open. She got it. She got it! That fast! Didn't they hear it? No one is moving to grab him! Why isn't anyone coming? Didn't they hear he just admitted he knocked off Robert Burgess? She just put her ass on the line in a bogus offer for kinky spanking to get this confession. Why aren't they moving?? Did she go too fast?

Shane smiles and whispers, "I am the man you think I am, perfectly capable of solving every problem and very anxious to solve yours. But right now, I'm not very hungry for dinner. I'm hungry to collect your very, very generous offer."

Her chest implodes. This game is free-falling to a new, low level and no one is coming to end it. Onyx necklace fail? Lipstick batteries low? She stares dazedly at Shane.

He gently places his napkin on the table. "I think we'd both be happier if we had room service in my suite. That lace dress is driving me crazy. The sooner we can be alone, the sooner I can get it off you and put my hands to better use."

She's frozen in a silent freak-out. If she leaves with Shane and his suite locks haven't been changed, her butt will be toast. Her life might be toast! Her fisted hands are in clear view on the table but Frank is too far away to notice. Frank wasn't supposed to rescue her anyway! She's equipped with two microphones! Everyone should be hearing this! People are supposed to come for her now!

She franticly develops Plan B. She'll fake a fall; that's it. She'll stand up now, twist her ankle, awkwardly fall and insist Frank take her home.

Suddenly, in the back of the restaurant, over Shane's left shoulder, Lauren sees movement. Three large men move in. People from one of the tables they just passed have gotten up and are walking over too. This is happening!

Lauren stops Shane from getting up, reaching for his hands.

"Wait. Maybe I'm not the woman *you* think I am," she whispers. "There is one thing you don't know."

He settles back in his chair and leans his head to the side, smiling and listening.

The approaching men are mere feet away.

She leans halfway over the table, the black lace from her dress pressing against the table linen. She's close enough to smell his cologne and feel her own breath on her fingers. She squeezes and kneads Shane's hands.

The men are coming closer.

"Nothing…" she whispers, drawing Shane to the edge of his chair. "…Nothing will ever come between me…and Andy."

She drops his hands.

The men arrive. "Shane Mitchell, you are under arrest."

An agent pulls Lauren's arm to get her the hell out of there.

Shane looks on in shock.

"What are you doing to her?" he yells, rising from the table. *"Let her go!"* An agent steps between them to block Shane's view while another agent subdues him.

The agent whisking Lauren away already has her near the bar, where Frank takes over. His arm wraps her body as they race through the door where Gregory is waiting. The three move quickly to the elevators.

"Did I get it? Did I get it?" Lauren breathlessly asks.

"They wouldn't have grabbed Shane if you hadn't," Frank says.

A Sand Club employee holds an elevator for them. They rush inside and Gregory pushes the eighth floor button.

"I got it? You sure I got it?" she repeats, panicked. What if it didn't work and Shane is coming after her right now? Oh God! He was ready to hit her!

She pounds the closed elevator doors as the cab rises, trying to move the elevator faster while her other hand yanks off her shoes. She's going to run like a wild woman down that hall to get to Andy.

Ding.

Eighth floor.

She bolts from the elevator, Frank behind her. Gregory fumbles to collect Lauren's shoes as he follows.

She turns the corner, running barefoot at full speed.

Down the hall, running towards her, is Andy.

He must have seen the commotion from his window and left the safety of the suite to meet her. His hair is blown back with the speed of his running, Lauren's short, lace dress inches higher with every step. Seeing each other moves them faster.

They crash together in a jubilant smash, their arms wrapping around each other as they spin. Her chin hits his shoulder but the pain is nothing compared to the overwhelming safety she feels in Andy's arms. She buries her head in his chest, smearing her eye makeup on his shirt.

"It's over? It's over? Did I do it? It's over?"

Andy pushes her back, breathless.

"You got it. It's done. It's over," he says calmly.

She screams with her tears, releasing a belly full of tension and frustration. She collapses against him and he gently lowers her to the ground, her legs bending as they sprawl together on the hallway floor.

"It's over," he whispers, rocking her as she wails. "It's all over."

Down the hall, Ryan stands outside the suite door.

On the other end of the long hallway, Frank and Gregory stand, Gregory clutching Lauren's Louis Vuitton black pumps.

They watch the collapsed heap of Andy and Lauren, rocking together on the floor in the middle of the hall.

Ryan looks down to Frank and raises one of his bruised hands.

Thumbs up.

Frank nods his agreement and returns the gesture.

Thumbs up.

[TWENTY]

The calm sound of quiet is all Lauren hears. She rolls over in bed, the sheets softly crinkling as her body turns. Andy's breathing is silent as he holds her, both of them lost in thought.

It will take a while for her to replay tonight's events in her mind. She's glad Andy wanted to stay in the suite at the Sand Club. For some strange reason, she's not ready to leave here yet.

Shane's last words haunt her. She keeps hearing his voice. *What are you doing to her; let her go.* He was worried about *her* in that moment, not himself. He always said he wanted to take care of her. He even thanked Frank tonight for watching her. How can a man have such different sides? He would do anything to protect her life, yet he was ready to take another man's life to do it. His touch brought her so much pleasure, yet he was ready to use his hand for an erotic round of dominance to give her pain. It's hard to imagine how bad this could have gone if she had started a new life with him. She would have been in danger if they ever disagreed. She could have been killed if she left him.

Tonight's sting caught Shane by surprise. Whoever gave him the tips about Doug and Ashley's wedding wasn't able to warn him. At some point, she will want to find out who had been talking to Shane, and why. Only Andy, Mary, Frank and Ryan knew what was really happening tonight. But Johnny didn't.

She remembers the sounds of lively music in a decorated barn and the crinkle of Amie's taffeta dress as she sat down beside her at Doug and Ashley's wedding. *I thought you and Shane made a great couple.* If Amie was such a fan, did she tip Shane to come to the wedding? Why?

For now, Lauren's trusted inner circle just got smaller. And to be safe, that circle doesn't include Amie's husband.

Soft light from Andy's phone on the bedside table brightens the room and interrupts her thoughts. He rolls over to read an incoming text.

"Who keeps texting?" She tries to tug his phone.

He puts it down. "Somebody."

There's another incoming text.

Andy rolls over again to read it, this time sitting up. He puts the phone down and turns to her. "Let's get dressed," he says, smiling.

"Is this an Andy Hayden surprise?"

He rolls out of bed and reaches for her hand.

"I promised you something. Now it's time to fulfill that promise." He tugs her gently out of bed.

Lauren pulls on a pair of jeans and a lightweight beige sweater that Andy had packed in an overnight bag. Her hair isn't styled; her makeup isn't on. Andy wears jeans and a t-shirt, reaching for her hand as they head for the door.

"Where are we going at 12:30 in the morning?" she asks, squeezing his hand. *They did this once before!* They must be heading to the beach to find a romantic spot to enjoy the night air.

Frank and Ryan come out of their room and join them in the hall.

"Oh, we get supervision too?" But neither Frank nor Ryan carries a towel or sheet to sit on. Maybe they aren't going to the beach?

Andy tightly holds her hand as they walk down the long hotel hallway. They pass the spot of their exuberant collapse, where a few hours ago they fell to this floor and celebrated the end of their ordeal with Shane. She scans the floor as they pass.

The elevator arrives, answering their down button call. By chance, this is the same elevator cab she rode in with Shane. Lauren squeezes

Andy's hand tighter. A few hours ago she pushed herself onto another man to flirt as part of the sting. Now she stands next to Andy, humbly holding his hand.

She still has no idea where they are going, except that they are going down.

The elevator doors open to the lobby, where they're greeted by the soft hum of floor-cleaning machines. The lobby is void of guests. Not even music plays while the hotel rests for the night. He leads her to the right, down the long marble hallway towards Saffron's restaurant.

Lauren glances at Andy's happy, smiling face.

"Why are you taking me back here?"

He squeezes her hand. "One way to get a memory out of your mind is to revisit where it took place. An even better way to remove a bad memory is to replace it with a good one."

Gregory stands under the yellow and black Saffron's sign, his jingling keys the only sound as he unlocks the restaurant door. He gives Lauren a warm smile. She returns his happy greeting.

Saffron's is dark. Only the lights under mirrors behind the bar help to guide their way. The delicious smell of served food lingers in the air, reminding her that she never did eat dinner last night. Andy and Lauren walk hand-in-hand through the restaurant, following Gregory.

Frank and Ryan stop at the bar. "We'll be waiting for you here," Frank says. Lauren nods.

Gregory leads them around the corner of the bar in a walk familiar to her. When she did this a few hours ago, she felt different. Shane held her bare back as she wore a dress to sell herself as someone he'd want to kill for. Now, her outfit doesn't need to sell any message. She's comfortable in her clothes, and very comfortable holding hands with Andy.

Lauren has a clear view of table number twenty-four. But now, the table is lit with several white candles, the sparse three roses now replaced with a glass vase of at least a dozen.

"Your table, Mr. Hayden."

"Thank you, Gregory."

Lauren stares at the table, at the chairs, remembering the intense stress. A few hours ago she needed to steer a conversation to get a confession. Shane's eyes faced her while the ears of law enforcement listened to every word they said. Now, only Andy can hear her.

"Where did you sit?" Andy asks, gesturing to the chairs. Lauren points to her spot and he pulls out her chair. He takes the seat across from her, where Shane sat.

She cautiously scans the dark restaurant. A red emergency exit sign lights up the back door where the men who arrested Shane came from. The eight-foot windows that frame this table are now lit with moonlight.

Love colors her gaze as she looks at the man sitting across from her now. What an improvement over last night.

"You wanted me to sit here and process this again, to get this out of my mind."

Andy nods. "Yes. Plus, I wanted to have a drink."

Clumsy sounds from Frank, Ryan and Gregory fooling around at the bar draw Lauren's smile.

"Are they our bartenders?"

"It's hard to find good help at this hour."

Soft, romantic candlelight casts a warm glow on Andy's face. His right eye looks much better but still shows signs of bruising. Even so, the sight of Andy across from her brings such joy.

"What a brilliant idea to come here. I'd rather fill my mind with the vision of you sitting across from me than the mental picture of the person I sat with last night."

Andy nods. "That was one reason I brought you here."

The rattling sounds from ice being tossed in a shaker are coming from the bar.

"Are you trying to get me drunk from these amateur bartenders?"

"That may be an outcome we both suffer."

Gregory approaches their table with two martinis, placing the glasses on the table. Lauren reaches for Gregory's hand.

"Andy and I have a little saying when we have a drink," she says. "A real friend would have given you a drink by now, and, looks like an old friend just did. Gregory, you are a real friend to us. Thank you for this now, what you did earlier tonight and everything you did to help me."

Gregory nods. "It's my pleasure to help special people, and the two of you are among my favorites." He steps away, then turns back. "But if you have any complaints about the quality of your drinks, direct them to those two guys who made them, not me," he says, laughing.

Lauren watches Andy smile at Gregory's joke. Andy's gone to such effort to arrange this creative, middle-of-the-night, memory-erasing night cap. God, she loves this man.

Their glasses gently clink in a soft toast. She drinks up the sight of his hazelnut-olive eyes as she sips.

"Mmmm, that's more like it," she says. "I promise I'm only drinking martinis now. My days of tequila shots are over!"

Andy laughs in agreement. Lauren glances down at her martini.

This flickering candlelight seems to be making the olives sparkle on her cocktail skewer. Really sparkle. She reaches down to pull the skewer higher. Threaded between two olives are her rings.

She lifts the skewer higher to see her diamond wedding and engagement rings and her silver ring, the rings she had given him to hold now dripping in martini.

"I promised I would hold them for you. And a real friend would have given you your rings back by now."

She holds up the dripping skewer. "Looks like my husband just did!"

She tugs at the olive on the end, laughing. "This is a two-hundred thousand dollar olive skewer!" she says, shaking her wet hand.

"Looks like you are dripping in diamonds."

She glances behind her, where Frank, Gregory and Ryan are watching them. "My martini had diamonds!" she yells. "I'll take another one of those!"

Andy frees the rings and dips them for a cleansing rinse in his glass of water. He reaches for her hands.

"Something occurred to me when you asked me to hold these rings," he says. "I gave you two of these rings here at the Sand Club."

"You're right! My silver ring you gave me on the beach and the engagement ring was in our suite!"

Andy nods. "After everything we've been through—I even had to give you this silver ring twice—here we are. Back at the Sand Club. And we are together."

He pushes her rings on her fingers and then gently holds her hands. "Until such time? Lauren, it will always be our time."

Tears blur her eyes. There is one place in the world she wants to be right now, and it's not in this chair so far from him. His eyes follow her as she quietly stands, moves around the table, and sits on his lap. Her hands stroke up his arms to his shoulders until she's holding him. His breath feels warm on her cheeks, the spicy leather smell of his cologne as comfortable as his hands now squeezing her back. "Andy, my time will always be with you."

Their lips meet for a kiss; lips that are a perfect match. Her soul fills with warmth. Again and again she indulges. Kissing Andy Hayden will never get old.

Their moment is interrupted by the unmistakable sounds of the cocktail mixer shaking up another round.

"Do you think that's for us or for them?" she asks.

"Hopefully there's enough for all of us."

"I'm up for another round."

"Lauren, I'm up for another round of life with you."

[TWENTY-ONE]

Three months later

Unseasonably cold temperatures chill the December air. Anytime the temperature dips into the 60s in Tampa it's considered downright cold. Right now, Lauren doesn't feel the chill, she feels the warmth of being surrounded by family.

She can't help but feel warm; her black Tahoe is packed with bodies right now.

"Mom," Aiden moans. "We really need a bigger car."

"I'm fine up here," Brittney brags, sitting next to Lauren in the middle row.

Andy sits on the other side of Lauren, his arm around his wife. He looks back to see what Aiden is complaining about. "You guys have grown, that's the problem."

Lee apparently hasn't heard a thing, nodding to the musical beat coming from his headphones.

Bill takes the steep curve exiting the interstate to head downtown to the Riverside Resort.

"Frank, are you sure you and Bill won't join us at our table for dinner tonight?" Lauren asks him again.

Frank is in his usual spot: front passenger seat. "Bill and I are fine eating at the bar. You deserve a nice, quiet birthday meal with your family."

Andy pats Lauren's shoulder. "It's not every day you turn forty."

"And today is not the day I turn it. I'm forty tomorrow."

"Hey, Mom," Lee says, his earbuds now removed. "Dad just texted. He wants to say 'hi' when we get there."

"Why am I not surprised Cory is working late on a Friday evening?" Lauren asks.

"Dad works late every evening," Aiden says.

Some things never change.

Bill approaches the entrance to the Riverside Resort. He slowly pulls under the covered entry, busy tonight with late-arriving guests checking into the hotel and those heading out for evening activities.

"So many memories here," Lauren says. "My first job was here, when I was in high school, with Davis!"

"Uncle Johnny worked here too," Lee adds. Aiden and Lee have added the honorary uncle title to all the Plebeian men, even Max.

Lauren leans towards the window so she can get a better look at the twenty-story glass front of the hotel. "Johnny asked me to start a band during an event here. This is where Plebeian was born."

"And look where that got you!" Brittney says. "I wouldn't be here with you if that hadn't happened!"

"Crazy things happen at the Riverside," Andy says.

Frank steps out of the car as Curtis, the longtime Riverside Resort doorman, opens Andy's door.

"Good evening, Logan and Hayden families!" Curtis says. "Mr. Logan mentioned you were dining at Gold Seasons tonight."

"Hi, Curtis," Lauren says, greeting him with a hug. The cold breeze nudges her black dress a little too far and she turns to tug it back down. "It's freezing tonight!"

"Anything under seventy degrees has always been cold to you," Curtis says, still holding the door open while Aiden and Lee unpack themselves from the third row.

Andy and Lauren lead the way into the hotel, Frank never more than three feet behind Lauren.

"Where did Cory say he'll meet us?" Lauren asks the boys.

"He said he's on the second floor," Lee reads from his phone.

They ride the grand escalator up, soft piano music filling the lobby. They turn to find Cory on the conference level.

"Hey!" Cory calls out, stepping out of the Gasparilla Ballroom. Lauren greets him with a hug.

"Hey, Andy and Brittney," Cory says, shaking their hands.

"Guys," Cory says, hugging Aiden and Lee, and fist bumping Frank.

"Happy birthday, Lauren," Cory says, his smile lighting up his face, those big blue eyes so unusually happy tonight.

"Tomorrow, everyone. My birthday is the 16th, not the 15th. I've got one more day!"

"She's trying to avoid the obvious," Andy says. "She just wanted to do a small dinner tonight then stay home all day tomorrow."

"Good plan," Cory says. "Then for your pre-birthday tonight, let me treat you to dinner. I've got your meal at Gold Seasons all set, my compliments."

"Thank you, Cory," she says, hugging him again. She really is a better friend to him than she ever was a wife. And he's a better friend to her than he ever was a husband. Tonight though, he sure is acting like a real friendly friend. "Would you like to join us?"

"Thanks, but I'm checking details for an event we have tomorrow," Cory says. "We just renovated this ballroom and a large dinner tomorrow night will be the first event here since renovation."

"I haven't been in the Gasparilla ballroom since our high school prom," Andy says, looking at Lauren.

Her eyes lower in a scolding stare. When they were in high school, Andy didn't take her to prom.

"We've added a new LED wave wall that illuminates with a choice of colored lighting. It's state-of-the-art," Cory says.

"Can I see?" Andy asks, always so curious to see features and designs of buildings. "We can look real fast."

"We have time. And we know enough people who work here. I'm not worried that they'll cancel our dinner reservation."

Bill has now joined them after parking the car and the group heads into the ballroom.

The room is dark and chilly but sure smells yummy, like baked chicken or something. Cory heads to a service panel. "From this one panel you can control everything now. All lights, air conditioning, sound…even surprises!"

He raises the light.

"Surprise!" screams a roomful of people.

Decorations in silver and gold cover the tables, with happy birthday balloons dancing in the air.

"No!" Lauren screams. *"No!"*

Andy has already backed away from her punching arms.

She punches Cory.

"Are you kidding me?" she yells.

"Gotcha, Mom!" Aiden cracks.

Lauren looks to Frank for answers. He shrugs. "I'm just glad this loud surprise didn't make you run."

"Happy birthday, Lauren," says a very familiar voice.

"Christy?" Lauren says with a squeal. She runs into her best friend's arms. She misses Christy's comforting arms and enthusiastic delight on life. Oh how she could have used Christy's company on this year's world tour. "Of course you had something to do with this!"

"Maybe just a little," Christy says. "I've felt so bad I couldn't be there with you on your summer tour. I begged for the time off work to come tonight!"

She looks around to see the room of friendly faces.

There are Doug and Ashley, Johnny and Amie and even Max! Michael and Sunny are all smiles, each holding one of Simone's hands as their pink, party dress-wearing toddler tries to twist free. Tish stands watch near the buffet tables while Oliver has apparently claimed the bar, drink in hand, with Mary smiling politely next to him. *Oh man, is he drinking again?* Lauren's mom and brother are here, as is Cindy, Andy's sister. Lynette and Lesley are here with their husbands and Ryan stands on the side of the room with his wife and Frank's wife. Even Josh is here, leaning on a cocktail table in the back. *Josh Spencer!*

"This isn't happening," Lauren says, spinning around to see all the faces, reaching to hug her mom and brother.

Andy pulls Lauren's arms and leads her into the center of the room.

"Happy birthday, baby," he says, kissing her. "I know you don't like surprises, but after the year you've had I thought you deserved a big birthday blowout."

"No kidding! What a year," she says, looking towards Johnny.

"So our party tonight is simple: food, drink, dance, cake and presents," Andy says. "And we're going to do it all backwards."

"Start with presents?"

"Presents first," Andy says, squeezing her arms.

"Seriously, I don't need anything. This is amazing; quite unexpected and amazing."

"No, Mom, we have presents!" Aiden says. "And we get to start."

Aiden, Lee and Brittney gather together. Guests clear a circle to watch.

Lee begins. "I know the house is lonely and empty since I've been gone to college."

"Lee, your dorm is twenty minutes from home. We see you all the time," Lauren says.

"Well, it's going to be empty when Brittney graduates this June and then Aiden a year later…"

Lauren turns to Andy for a celebratory fist-bump.

"Mom!" Aiden says.

Lee continues. "And the three of us, well, we have our own projects we are going to be working on when we move out."

Johnny hollers from the middle of the room. "Not the LAB band!"

"Oh yes!" Brittney says, sending him a scolding look. "We have a band and we are good. One day, if you ever give us a chance, we'll play for you!"

Lee finishes, "So while we are off to college and making ourselves famous with our first album, Chocolate Lab, we thought she could keep you company."

"She?" Lauren asks.

Tish brings out a little brown puppy.

"A puppy?!" Lauren shrieks. "You are replacing yourselves with…a puppy?!"

"Not just any puppy," Aiden says, taking the puppy from Tish and bringing her to Lauren. "She's a chocolate lab!"

Lauren is laughing so hard she can hardly move. Andy shakes his head beside her. Aiden hands her the puppy, adorned with a pink collar and matching bow. The puppy licks Lauren's hands and tries to lick her face.

"See why we need a bigger car!" Aiden says.

"I can't believe this," Lauren says. "Thank you, guys. Does she have a name?"

"She does!" Brittney says.

Lauren looks to Andy, scared to ask what the name is. They've probably named this chocolate lab a chocolate-themed name to go with their Chocolate Lab album idea.

"We wanted it to be special, something you love. So even when she chews your expensive shoes you can't be mad when you yell her name!" Lee says.

Lauren shakes her head. She cannot imagine what these kids have named this dog.

"Okay, what's the puppy's name?"

Lee smiles. "Cabo."

Lauren turns to Andy. "Cabo!"

Andy reaches to pet Cabo and welcome her to the family. "Now I have another girl in the house!"

Lauren puts Cabo down to let her play. Simone quickly toddles over to watch the puppy.

Lauren pulls Lee, Aiden and Brittney together for a hug. "I'm going to love Cabo as much as I love each of you; maybe even more," she says, winking. "Seriously, I love you. Thank you very much."

"Okay, so there are two more gifts," Andy says, "and they are both from me."

"Two?" What could Andy possibly give her?

"My first gift is Todd Peppers," Andy says.

Lauren turns to see the tan skin, white-enameled smile and built biceps of the former football player, now Plebeian's trusted lawyer, standing nearby. His slender, beautiful, blonde wife is at his side.

"I get Todd as a gift? Is this a one-night gift or do I get to keep him forever?"

"We'll go with one night. My hourly rate goes up at forever," Todd says, smiling. He gives her a hug. "Happy birthday, Lauren."

"Your hands are empty, so no second puppy?"

Todd smiles. "Actually, Cabo is the perfect comparison to the gift I do have for you. You sure weren't looking for a puppy, but everyone here knows you will love Cabo."

Lauren nods, not exactly sure where this is going.

"That is the same thing that happened with Plebeian. You weren't looking for fame, but after you adjusted to it, being in Plebeian was something that you loved."

She nods, scanning the room to find Johnny.

"As we all know, Plebeian disbanded earlier this year in a dispute with Platinum Plate records. The legal path we were taking to end ties with Platinum Plate has now changed since Shane Mitchell disappeared."

Lauren stiffens hearing Shane's name. Not even Johnny knows about her role in Shane's arrest, and no one ever will. In fact, right now, even she, Andy and Frank don't know what's happened to Shane since that night. It's like the FBI has made him completely disappear.

Todd continues. "Platinum Plate was still under Shane's ownership until recently. The company has been liquidated. All assets have been sold."

Oliver nudges Lauren. "Nothing like a bunch of legal talk to kill the buzz of a party." She swats at him.

Todd continues. "Platinum Plate does not exist anymore, nor do any contracts they held. Your birthday gift is simple: there is nothing now that would prohibit the band Plebeian from getting back together."

"Really?"

"Really," he says.

"No legal problems?"

"You can use your original name and there are no legal problems," Todd says.

"It could start again, just like before?"

"Just like before."

The only sounds in the quiet ballroom come from the playful growls of Cabo, now tugging on a cloth napkin with Simone.

Lauren looks at Andy. "It could start again?"

Andy nods. "It could. But only *if* you could find some people that wanted to be in the band."

She turns to look for the guys. The room remains quiet.

Then Michael steps forward, standing in the center of the circle of friends.

"My baby eats a lot," Michael says, drawing laughter from their friends. "And it looks like I'm going to have to buy her a puppy next. It wouldn't hurt for me to earn some extra cash. I'll be Plebeian's keyboardist."

Doug steps forward with a massive grin on his face. He raises an eyebrow and looks to Michael. "Doug's in," Michael says.

Lauren couldn't remove the smile from her face if she tried.

Max steps forward and stands next to Michael and Doug.

"I barely got started on tour before I fell off the stage," Max says, smiling. "I'd sure like another shot at being Plebeian's rhythm guitarist."

Lauren's hands are on her face. She's not surprised these guys want to form a band again yet she can't believe this is happening right now!

Oliver slaps his bony hand on her shoulder. "Plebeian needs me more than I need Plebeian. But right now, I have nothing better to do. Sign me up for bass guitar."

Davis walks forward. "No, no, no. I know these people. They don't know what they are doing. They'll need a manager for this band. Now that's something I can do."

Movement from the back draws everyone's eyes. Lynette and Lesley are making their way to the front. "I can make up a whole new set of situation codes to handle the next chapter of Plebeian. Sign both of us up as your publicists," Lynette says.

In the middle of the room, Trent raises his hand. "I just got the world tour cleaned up but I'm good to go for another one when Plebeian is ready. You got me as production manager."

Frank moves in from the side of the room, nodding for Ryan to join him. "We've been hurt in car accidents, beaten by thugs, seen most of you drunk and witnessed some other things we probably shouldn't repeat with the kids here," Frank says. "You keep things exciting, though largely unsafe, and I can't imagine a better job. If Plebeian is coming back together, Ryan and I would be honored to protect all of you, just like we do for your family."

Smiles fill the room as Plebeian is rebuilt, one talented person at a time.

Finally, Johnny's smiling face comes forward. Seeing him makes the tears she was holding back start to joyously flow. He moves past the gathering group to step the closest to Lauren.

"You and I started this whole thing, right here at the Riverside. I convinced you to sing six songs for a movie soundtrack. I promised you our band would never be revealed. So I got more than six songs from you and a few people found out about us, huh?"

She nods, sniffling.

"Plebeian was more than my dream. Plebeian became my family."

Johnny looks at the others. "I got my dream. But I miss my family. If this thing is going to go another round, you know damn well I'll be the lead guitarist."

Oliver pats Johnny's back in a congratulatory slap.

Lauren shakes her head like a proud mother while tears streak down her face.

There's her ex-college boyfriend, Johnny.

Her son's former percussion teacher, Doug.

Her church's former organist, Michael.

And the guy she kind of can't stand, Oliver.

All standing next to Max, the son of their first, and murdered, record producer.

They're all looking at her now.

Lauren's ride on Plebeian had been over. There were no more grueling tours, no more rancid smells of spilled beer in crowded arenas. No more media interviews, costume fittings or the clay-mask feel of stage makeup. There were no more critical eyes or creepy guys staring at her with their hands down their pants. She didn't need sunglasses to hide her insecurities. Finally, rumors of her and Johnny getting back together had stopped.

While she misses some things, she really enjoys just being Lauren Hayden.

Putting Plebeian back together now would be different. She's older. People her age don't make it in this business. She and Johnny only made it the first time because of their clever marketing as unknowns. Will fans even want to buy records from a band with a forty-year-old singer and lead guitarist? Rock bands become overnight, has-beens in this business. How can they pick up the momentum they had from a few months ago?

She looks to her right and sees Andy's smiling face. Fame opened the path to her high school crush. Their journey hasn't been smooth, but after everything, Andy is still here.

Next to Andy stand his daughter, now her daughter, and her two sons. Fame brought their blended family together, with squabbles and arguments, laughter and love. The kids are trying to follow in her footsteps with a band of their own but is she really, *really* ready to turn over the home studio to them?

She looks out to her friends. All of them are smiling or nodding for her to say something.

"Come on, Chipper!" Max says.

Johnny, Michael and Doug are nodding. Oliver is the only one who isn't. He looks grumpy, maybe mad. Pretty much like usual. He steps forward. "You're scared of the stares and don't like being on stage. Who cares? Get over it and get back on board." He smiles.

She dabs her eyes dry. "You're right. I don't like people staring at me. I don't think I'm anything special. But I do like most of you. I'm not going to miss an opportunity for another ride. What the heck! I'm in as lead singer!"

Andy opens his arms to Lauren. "Good call," he whispers, holding her.

Lauren moves to the center of the group where she, Johnny, Doug, Michael, Oliver and Max link arms to form their traditional huddle.

Their heads lower together. "Let's make more beautiful, marketable music," Johnny says.

"And you know what? I just got a great, new idea on how to do it!" Lauren says.

A chorus of "ohhhh" rumbles from the guys in the huddle.

Plebeian has been reborn and the party just got started.

But Davis's yell interrupts them.

"*Whoa, whoa, whoa!*" Davis yells. "We are missing something!"

Michael breaks away from the huddle, throwing his hands in the air. "You're right!"

Doug nods.

Lynette adds, "We can't move forward without it!"

Oliver says, "Huge problem. Just huge."

Lauren stands in the middle, watching everyone bat around some imaginary problem. "What are you talking about?"

Johnny shakes his head. "We had it before and we'll need another one now."

"But, where will we get one this time?" Max says.

This is cute. Confusing, but cute.

Andy reaches for her hand, pulling her closer. "I've got the answer to your problem."

What problem? What answer?

He smiles. "This is the second part of your birthday gift." His smiling face goes serious, he squeezes her hands. He looks down to the floor, then back up to her eyes. A blanket of quiet covers the room.

"I had to watch you struggle on world tour and there was little I could do for you," he quietly says.

The struggle was real, but where is this going?

"Now that Shane is out of the picture, I finally figured out a way that I could help. It's something you are going to need. Something Shane offered you before." He whispers in her ear, "And it's my own way of taking a final shot at Shane."

Her head is spinning. *What is?*

"Todd?" Andy asks, dropping Lauren's hands.

Todd steps forward again, holding a large manila envelope.

She scans the room. So many smiles. So many nervous-looking expressions. Everyone seems to be on the brink of eruption—this surprise party has so many surprises!

"Lauren," Todd says, "Andy has used his considerable connections in the financial arena to assemble a group of private investors. Together, they formed a company. To be specific, a new record company that you and Andy now control."

"What?!" She spins to Andy, who wears the biggest "gotcha" grin of his life. "We have our own record company?"

He nods. "Not only is Platinum Plate gone, but we've replaced them with a brand new label: Hayden Productions."

"Are you serious?"

"And," Todd says, "Hayden Productions has made a substantial investment purchasing all licenses previously owned by Platinum Plate. Hayden Productions now has complete ownership and control of the licenses for Plebeian music that Platinum Plate once owned. You have your own record company and you own your own music."

"Andy!" Lauren screams, throwing herself at him and drawing wild cheers and applause from their friends. The sudden burst of noise scares Simone so much she starts to cry. Hugs and high-fives fill the room.

Lauren and Andy spin in a circle, tight in their embrace.

"You always find a way to win," she whispers. "This, though, this tops anything you've ever done!"

Andy whispers, "In the words of my arrested adversary, there's no problem I can't solve."

"Once again, you, Andy Hayden, are my hero."

Her lips press to his again as the party comes alive.

Music plays and people congratulate each other. A toddler screams in one corner and across the room, a playful puppy barks. Silver lids lift from chafing dishes as the buffet opens and drinks flow from the open bar.

Lauren exchanges hugs with everyone, squeezing Doug, Michael, Max and Oliver the hardest. She's surrounded by laughing, embracing and celebrating. Andy has already made his way across the room, holding high the manila envelope with the documents that form their new record company.

Her face hurts from smiling. This is the best birthday ever!

She turns to hug the next person and notices Johnny, now coming closer.

He's not screaming like the others. His smile is simple, humble.

They come face to face.

"Plebeian is back! Here we go again," she says, reaching for his hands. "And our own record company too!"

"It's a dream come true; another journey with you," Johnny says.

His smile says so much more right now, so many messages.

"We've taken some incredible journeys together," she says, squeezing his hands.

"The best of my life."

Noisy celebration surrounds them, yet Johnny and Lauren stand still, drawn together in a familiar but odd pull.

Very odd.

She turns her head, trying to read Johnny's eyes. Usually they can look at each other and understand what the other is saying. Right now he looks like he's saying…

Can't be. She hasn't seen that look in years. She drops his hands and steps back.

But he reaches for her, one hand tenderly squeezing her shoulder.

She quickly tries to process what his eyes are saying.

It's something he used to say before.

And something he's not supposed to say now.

"I love you, Lauren. I always have, and I always will."

Other Books by Debbie K. Lum

PLEBEIAN REVEALED (BOOK ONE)

When Lauren Logan, an introverted wife and mother, records a secret movie soundtrack with her ex-boyfriend, she gets more than sudden fame when their band Plebeian is revealed.

PLEBEIAN REBORN (BOOK THREE)

Lauren Hayden has survived remarkable challenges as the lead singer of Plebeian. Now she faces her biggest challenge yet—her mistakes from the past. When tragedy strikes and secrets are revealed, she unravels in a downward spiral. Only one man can save her, and Plebeian, now.

THE DOCTOR, THE CHEF OR THE FIREMAN

A small-town girl running from a big-time secret finds herself in the middle of danger, and in the arms of an unexpected love.

I CAN HANDLE HIM

Quinn Corbin's got nothing to lose – except her life.

She's finally got the attention of the man she's always loved, Nick Allen. But Nick has a reputation for trouble. And after a car explosion killed his last girlfriend, many people in San Antonio, Texas think Nick got away with murder.

But Quinn, a twenty-four-year-old elementary school teacher and bubbly optimist, believes Nick is innocent. So does her best friend Tory, a law student and sarcastic realist. Soon Quinn and Nick find their relationship growing when suddenly their world upends. Now Nick is in major trouble again and Quinn may have made the biggest mistake of her life.

With incriminating evidence mounting against Nick, Tory works to prove his innocence. But Nick finds himself in a bigger battle when he must fight to protect, and win, his true love.

About the Author

Debbie Krueger Lum has enjoyed a 28-year professional career in marketing, where she loved turning big, complicated problems into smooth, organized programs. She's travelled from the beaches of Turkey, to the volcanoes in Italy to the bricks of Red Square, Moscow. And no one can drink more unsweetened iced tea than her.

After seeing a self-esteem campaign encouraging little girls to dream big, she wondered why not grown women too? She challenged herself to do something she knew little about: reading and writing novels.

PLEBEIAN IN DANGER is her second novel, second in the PLEBEIAN series.

www.debbielum.com

www.ingramcontent.com/pod-product-compliance
Lightning Source LLC
Chambersburg PA
CBHW031239210726
48287CB00003B/822